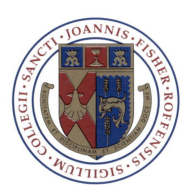

Magdalena

Cecilia Manguerra Brainard

Plain View Press
P. O. 33311
Austin, TX 78764

plainviewpress.com
sbright1@austin.rr.com
1-800-878-3605

Acknowledgements

Portions of this novel have appeared in *"Mirror Weekly"*; *"Sunstar Weekend"*; *"The Philippine Graphic"*; On a Bed of Rice: An Asian American Erotic Feast (Anchor Book, 1995); Forbidden Fruit (Anvil, 1992); and Babaylan: An Anthology of Filipina and Filipina American Writers (Aunt Lute, 2000)

Also by Cecilia Manguerra Brainard

Acapulco at Sunset and Other Stories
Contemporary Fiction by Filipinos in America (editor)
Fiction by Filipinos in America (editor)
Journey of 100 Years: Reflections on the Centennial of Philippine
    Independence (co-editor)
Philippine Woman in America
When the Rainbow Goddess Wept (Song of Yvonne)
Woman With Horns and Other Stories

For

Lauren, Chris, Alex and Drew Brainard

Contents

Prologue

Soon after I found out I was pregnant, I decided to write my mother's story. I never actually knew her although all my life I'd heard about her. She was not someone real, but was the nighttime stories of my grandmother, the wistful anecdotes my *Tiya* Estrella would sometimes relate. She was the faded photograph of a cautious-looking woman with a wistful smile, good-looking, yes, but with a strain around her eyes and lips. She was the bundle of letters, photographs, and journals that my grandmother kept at the bottom of her armoire. She was bits and fragments of words and paper and cellulose — ethereal, a ghost I could not pin down.

I'd grown up knowing my mother died at the delivery table, and it wasn't until I was in school when I realized that the other children's mothers hadn't died during childbirth. Once I had asked my grandmother about that; I had asked her if I'd killed my mother. "No," she had said. "No, it was not your fault."

"Then whose fault was it?" I asked.

"Her father's family is to blame."

I was young then and spent a lot of time wondering how my grandfather and his family killed her. I used to badger my grandmother for information about the Sanchez family, but all I got was that they were a wealthy bunch. Before she died, my grandmother did tell me the truth about my mother's real father. Finally, I understood the reason behind her lack of forthrightness, why for decades she had kept this a secret.

A secret has tremendous power. My grandmother had used her secret as a weapon, but the strange thing is the secret in turn possessed her, held her captive. For years, she guarded her secret carefully, never thinking, never expecting that her own daughter would have the same sort of secret.

My mother's secret had to do with who my father was. For years my grandmother refused to talk about him. She looked at men as irrelevant in the matter of childbearing — I sprung from my mother's womb, and my mother had sprung from hers. But I knew early on that I wasn't just my mother's daughter, that someone else's blood coursed through my veins. I could see it in my pale skin and the hazel sparks of my eyes; and I could see it in the faces of people who stared at me in a knowing way. Sometimes when I glanced at the mirror in semi-darkness, I could see his shadow fleeting across my face and sometimes I tried to catch him, but my hands met only the frightened face of my mother's daughter.

My *Tiya* Estrella gave me pictures of my father. From her I learned my father had been an American captain stationed in Mactan during the Vietnam War; and I found out that his plane was shot down while on a mission in Vietnam.

When I felt life within me, I felt it was time to turn their secrets into stories. And so I started writing. I started out writing about my mother, then my grandmother, and to my surprise about other family members. They would come to me in dreams and thoughts, when I least expected it, begging to have their stories written, to have their secrets revealed. Even they must have realized it was time to release those festering secrets once and for all.

I have done my best; I have used whatever guile in storytelling I know to record their stories. It is done. I am ready. When this child in my belly will come to me and say, "Tell me . . . " then he can have it all, everything I know about these people whose blood he carries within himself.

Juana

8

The Family

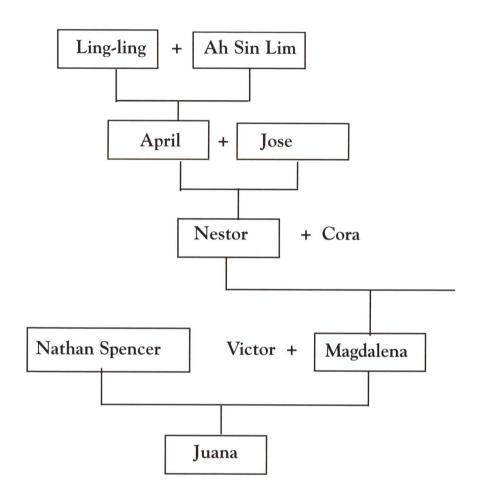

Ling-ling + Ah Sin Lim

April + Jose

Nestor + Cora

Nathan Spencer   Victor + Magdalena

Juana

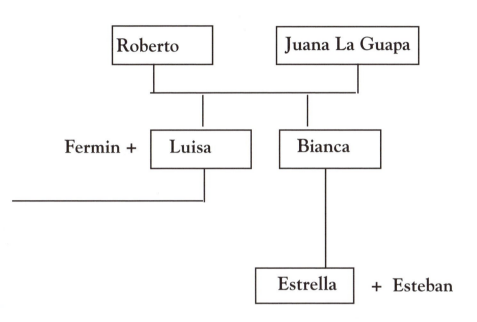

Roberto — Juana La Guapa

Fermin + Luisa   Bianca

Estrella + Esteban

11

Magdalena by the Sea
(1966-67)

From the start Magdalena had refused to see Victor for what he really was. On their honeymoon, in Baguio, he had left her in the morning to order breakfast, or so he said, and Magdalena had waited for a long time in their bedroom, until at last she went down to find Victor having a cup of coffee with a good-looking American woman. Magdalena had stood by the entrance of the coffee shop, with her hand to her mouth, uncertain about what to do. Victor gave some story about the poor tourist not knowing what places to see in Baguio, and Magdalena believed him.

Later, when there were other incidents with women, far more flagrant, Magdalena continued to believe Victor. There was a time when Victor would recklessly date his women in clubs and restaurants. They were always young and pretty, but regardless, Magdalena would entertain Victor's line about how the women were simply having family problems and needed his advice.

For five years, Magdalena put up with Victor. She acquired some weapons along the way. She knew she couldn't afford to look like a loser, so she dressed impeccably in expensive designer clothes. Her hair was always perfectly coiffed; her fingernails and toenails were always painted her favorite pallid pink color. Her face wore the powdery perfection of Helena Rubenstein. If her lips looked a bit tight around the edges and her eyes bore the expression of a dog that had been kicked around, at least her overall appearance exuded wealth, aloofness, and arrogance. It was the same look other society matrons had. She had mastered her denial so well that anyone talking to her would leave wondering if indeed they had misjudged Victor, the unfortunate and caring son of a tobacco merchant.

In late 1966 however, Magdalena's mother, Luisa, invited Magdalena to lunch and spelled out some new details about Victor: he had a mistress; in fact, they lived together in Mandawe, a block away from the church, right beside the Botica Boie; the other woman had been a nightclub performer; and worst of all Victor and this woman had an infant son.

Magdalena's blood turned into molasses. Her first instinct was to cover-up, and she declared it was all just tawdry gossip, and why should her mother listen to such nonsense. Luisa pointed out that it had been six months since Victor moved out of his and Magdalena's bedroom and into their cabaña; and that during that time he and Magdalena had been going their own way, he with his rattan furniture factory, she with her monkey farm.

Chills ran up and down her spine. Through a kind of fog, she heard her mother insisting that she ask Victor back to spare her the humiliation of being a separated woman. "Offer the woman money, insist that he come home, you are his wife after all. The worst thing that could happen is for you to end up a separated woman. People will ridicule you," Luisa said. "I cannot understand how Victor could do this to us. He was nothing, nothing. But I knew, from the first time I laid eyes on him, I knew he would give you tears. Do you remember, I specifically told you, 'Magdalena, mark my words, this man will be your cross to bear.'"

Before her mother could continue, Magdalena got up and left her mother's house. She was furious. It was unthinkable that Luisa would spread such destructive gossip. Her mother was a cruel and flighty woman; that was it. Magdalena's mind fixed on her childhood when Luisa hardly spent time with her. It was Magdalena's father who had pampered her. Fermin had read fairy tales to her at bedtime; and Fermin had bought her the frilly clothes from Escolta. Luisa had always been too busy with her volunteer work and her orchids. From the time Magdalena could remember, Luisa was a distant, cold, and terrible mother.

Back in her own home in Mactan Island, Magdalena locked herself in her room. Lying spread-eagle on her bed, she stared at the faint water stain on her ceiling. She discovered that if she did not blink her eyes the stain took on strange designs, first a blob, then a three-legged cat, then a crooked cactus tree. When the stain took on the form of a curled-up fetus, she wept. A few months after she had married Victor, she had miscarried, and she never got pregnant again. This memory rushed back to her, and the thought of Victor having a child with this other woman gave her pain she had never experienced before.

She wept all through the night until dawn when she glanced out her window and saw the faint golden glow of the sky. She dried her eyes and blew her nose. A glimmer of hope flickered in her heart:

perhaps her mother had made a mistake, perhaps it had all been untrue. She decided to check the cabaña, which was a separate wing of her sprawling bungalow. She searched the bookcase for Victor's beloved motorcycle trophies, and heaved a deep sigh when she saw that they were gone.

Before the sun was up, she was out walking briskly along the seashore, breathing in the clean sea air. She looked at the tranquil bay fronting her house and perhaps it was the beauty of the sea that made her mind concoct another excuse for Victor. She imagined that Victor was the victim of this woman, that she was a hardcore whore who had blackmailed Victor or who had some kind of unearthly hold on him. She pictured her as a cheap, heavily made-up hussy, with long hair down to her buttocks, just like the painted women who hung around the American Base in Mactan. And she remembered Victor during his contrite times when he begged for her forgiveness, all softness and tenderness. He would even cry, the poor man. After all, he had come from a broken home; he had had very little opportunities. She wept once again, this time for Victor's sorrowful past that invaded her being, saturating every cell of her body with deep melancholia.

On Sunday, she drove to Mandawe. She had it all planned. She would go to his other house and demand to see him. Her very presence would knock some sense into his head and he would beg for forgiveness. He would return home with her, and life would be fine once again — or at least as fine as it had been for the past five years. It seemed like a sensible plan.

She set out and was so intent on her mission that she missed seeing a large hole in the sidewalk. Magdalena twisted her left leg and fell down. Her purse flew open; her things lay scattered around. She tried to get up, wincing at the pain, when she heard a woman's voice asking if she needed help. A young woman with a baby in her arms helped Magdalena up, and the stranger gathered her things and handed them to her. "The sidewalk is bad," the woman said, "Come in, come into my home, you need to put ice on your ankle or else it'll swell. When I was twelve, I fell off a jeepney and hurt myself. An older woman helped me. I've never forgotten her." She flashed a smile at Magdalena.

Magdalena limped toward the house next to Botica Boie. It came to her that this was Victor's mistress. She was nothing at all like the painted woman in her imagination; this woman was plain and dressed simply. Magdalena looked at the baby with its round, pleasant face. "His name is Inocencio," the woman said, tickling the baby's chin. "He's only a month old. He looks like my father. Look at that, just like a little old man. He's dead now. He died two years ago of cholera. We lived in Tondo, and epidemic there can be bad."

Any thought of seeing Victor flew from Magdalena's mind. She became flustered. Then she considered entering the house just to see what it looked like, to see what Victor's other house was like, to get an inkling of what his other life was all about. But she knew that such details would only feed her imagination, would only drive her mad. In front of the gate, Magdalena stopped. "I'm sorry," Magdalena said, "I have to go." And as quickly as she could, she hobbled back to her car.

It was Victor who came to see her. He stopped by one day when the president and vice-president of the Catholic Women of the Virgin Mary Most Pure were visiting. The women, friends of Luisa, were soliciting Magdalena's help for their May fund-raiser. Their eyes lit up when they heard the roar of Victor's motorcycle, and they eyed each other nervously when Victor barged into the front door and struggled to remove his helmet.

"Victor," Magdalena said faintly. She folded her hands over her heart. The two women faded away and only Victor stood before her. She forgot all about the other woman and the baby and saw a man who symbolized a vague and pleasant past, a time when she was young and could dream of infinite possibilities. Specifically, she remembered the time she had cut class to meet Victor in front of the university carillon tower. They had climbed up the narrow, winding stairs of the tower to the very top. She had stared at the surrounding vast fields, at the azure sky, at the emerald leaves and red flowers of the nearby flame trees. Victor had held her away from the ledge for fear she would fall, his warm hands resting on her waist. They had kissed, and the world had seemed so vibrant, so clear, and Magdalena had felt so sure of herself, so sure of what love was, of Victor's love. Now, she stared at Victor and experienced hope. He had come back to her. Things could still be worked out between them. "Victor," she repeated, as if she would swoon, feeling as if the world around her had turned into water, shimmering around her, passing her by.

Victor threw his helmet on a chair and said, "Magdalena, I want to talk to you."

He headed for the bedroom; Magdalena followed. Before she had the chance to close the door, Victor shouted, "Magdalena, I heard you went to Mandawe. This kind of scandal doesn't work, Magdalena. I don't want you ever, ever going to that house again!"

"But-but Victor . . . " Magdalena stammered, in a hollow, tinny voice, her mind still up that carillon tower.

"Just keep her out of this, Magdalena! She's a young girl. When she realized it was you, she was so upset she had to see the doctor. Leave her alone."

His words bounced around the bedroom and echoed down the hallway to the living room where two women sat breathlessly listening.

Pacing back and forth, his energy brimming over, Victor went on, "I won't have it. It's unthinkable. She and the baby are the only good things in my life. Leave them alone."

By now Magdalena had left the carillon tower and found herself in some other moment in the past, reading Victor's love letter to a girl named Mila. Bolstered by the anger of that memory, Magdalena found herself speaking, "Leave them alone? You won't have it? And who am I? Am I not your wife? Don't I have rights? You never even had the decency to tell me. I had to find out from my mother!" Magdalena slapped Victor.

With his left hand, he held her; with his right, he struck her. Magdalena pulled away, and completely forgetting the two women in the living room, she opened the bedroom door and ran to the hallway. "Don't you dare touch me! You and your women. You have given me more pain than any person ever has. Get out!"

Victor froze, stunned at her rage. For a long while, they stared at each other.

"Magdalena," he finally said, "I'm sorry. I don't know what got into me. Things have been so complicated. I'm sorry. Listen, I don't want to hurt you."

"You have done nothing but hurt me. From the start, you have hurt me. And now this woman with this child. You cannot imagine my anguish, not only because I know you're with someone else but because I feel like a failure."

"Magdalena, I'm sorry. Believe me when I say I'm sorry. It's not you. It's the whole thing. It hasn't worked out between us. From the start your parents disliked me, and they made sure I knew it. Do you remember when we talked about moving to Manila? We should have,

Magdalena. We should have moved far away. I never felt I belonged here in this home your parents gave you. That was made very clear to me, you know, that this house and property belong to only you. Everything around here belonged to you — your family, your high-society friends, even the house and properties are yours. It's not that I wanted those things, but I owned nothing. People called me 'Magdalena's husband.' How do you think that made me feel? At least, I'm happy now. I have a home, a woman who loves me, a son."

Sucking her breath in, Magdalena moved away from Victor. He followed.

They found themselves in the living room where the two women sat pale and silent.

Victor turned to them. "You two had better not talk to anyone about this!"

The women gasped and retreated to the door.

"Please don't leave. I have more rice cakes. Sit down, please," Magdalena pleaded.

Meantime, Victor had grabbed his helmet and had left.

Patting Magdalena's arm, the women lingered, assuring Magdalena they would keep matters to themselves; and then they left.

Magdalena watched them waving from their car, and she knew that the second they got back to their homes, they would be on the phones to tell everybody what had happened. "*Madre de Dios*, you'll never believe . . . " they would start before they launched into their story about the awful fight she and Victor had.

Magdalena owned a monkey farm on a piece of property near the American Air Force Base. Victor had started the monkey farm shortly after he learned that American laboratories bought monkeys for experimentation, and that they paid in dollars. He had hired trappers who penetrated dense forests to capture the unfortunate animals. When Victor started a rattan factory, he lost interest in the monkey farm, and gradually Magdalena took over management. Too much money had been invested in the business, she had said, and she couldn't let it go to waste.

After Victor's catastrophic visit, to hide from people's probing eyes and sharp tongues, she spent most of her time at the monkey farm. During this time an incident occurred that affected Magdalena tremendously.

A rush order for a baby monkey arrived from a local client, the Ubec Scientific Laboratory. Magdalena handed the order to the caretaker, Raymundo, who said there was only one baby, a six-week-old male, unweaned who clung to his mother's chest.

Raymundo thought it would be an easy matter, and he reached into the cage to try and grab the mother, but she grew wild and bit his hand. Two men had to prod her with sticks and trick her out of the cage. With one protective hand over her baby, the mother furiously snapped and growled. Unable to handle her, one of the men finally lassoed her around the neck. Her breath cut short, the mother released the baby, and a man quickly yanked the startled baby away. Still clutching a tuft of her mother's gray hair, the baby shrieked and howled while the gagging mother quivered and foamed at the mouth. For a long time the mother fought valiantly to get her baby back, but the rope restrained her well, and soon the mother was back in her cage, and the baby packed off to the lab.

It was the first time Magdalena saw such a spectacle. She told Raymundo to give the mother extra food, but the animal flung the papaya at him. For three solid hours, the animal screamed and hurled herself against the cage walls, until finally Magdalena could not stand the racket and left.

Back home, she lay exhausted on her bed. The image of the mother clawing for its baby loomed in her mind. Something else surfaced in her consciousness — the memory of her unborn child. No matter how hard she tried to shake it off, there it was, the miscarriage, the blood, the sadness, the wondering about the child. She tried hard to push it away from her thoughts; but the harder she tried, the more exhausted she became until she finally fell asleep.

Magdalena dreamt of the first time she and Victor met at the Club Filipino. It was New Year's eve. Magdalena — eighteen and very excited but also feeling hopelessly plain beside the scintillating girls of Ubec with their rouged cheeks and ruffled dresses. Victor — pomaded, thick arching eyebrows, handsome, brash. He asked her to dance the tango. In her dream, Magdalena could hear the pulsing music all over again. She could feel the warm, humid breeze that rustled through the open balcony doors. She smelled the oily sweet scent of Victor's pomade. She didn't know how to tango, but Victor told her not to worry, and he led her well. As he stared at Magdalena with intense dark eyes, he murmured: "I looked at all the girls here and saw you. I told myself, that's the girl for me. There's no comparison between you and the rest. You're incredibly beautiful."

Incredibly beautiful! It was the first time any man said those words to Magdalena, and she lowered her eyes, and embarrassment and happiness both flooded her soul. But after flirting with her, Victor turned his attention to Miss Ubec with the strapless hourglass gown. Magdalena sat there, watching them from the corner of her eye, feeling hurt, confused; and yet, something had happened to her. This debonair bachelor had called her beautiful, had given her attention, and for the first time, Magdalena felt like a grown woman — an incredibly beautiful woman.

She awoke with a parched throat and the realization that Victor was gone, and that indeed a portion of her life had turned into nothing more than intangible memories.

Later she called the office and asked Raymundo to get back the baby monkey. Raymundo said it was too late, that the monkey was dead by now. She returned to the monkey farm to visit the mother monkey that lay still in a corner of her cage. At first Magdalena thought the monkey was dead, and Raymundo had to prod her with a stick and the monkey had to growl before Magdalena believed the monkey was still alive. "I'm sorry," Magdalena said, "I'm sorry for what I've done to you."

Turning to Raymundo, she instructed, "Put her in a small cage, I'm taking her home."

Raymundo placed the monkey in a chicken-wire cage, warning her to be careful because the monkey might bite and rabies among monkeys was not uncommon. Magdalena was not afraid; she only felt strong resolution to make the monkey well.

She kept the cage in her room and skipped supper entirely — she was so busy fussing with the animal. She placed newspapers under the cage, which she kept beside her bed. She offered the monkey a variety of fruit but the animal refused to eat. Later, instead of reading the magazines piled up on her side-table, she continued her vigil. She slept lightly; the few times she dozed off, she'd wake up with a start, thinking the monkey was dead. She'd snap on the light and peer into the cage, and sigh with relief that the monkey was still alive.

Early the next morning, she summoned the carpenter and told him to build a small house with a bamboo pole running horizontally alongside, so the monkey would have shelter in the verandah. Once the monkey was situated in its new home, she spent most of her time studying the monkey, thinking about her, its baby, and feeling desperately sad. The monkey had lost her baby; and she was wasting away from sorrow.

Stroking the monkey, Magdalena whispered, "You will die if you don't eat. You will die."

Magdalena went to the kitchen and selected a perfect ripe mango. She peeled it and cut up the flesh unto a small plate. Returning to the verandah, she hand-fed the monkey that spat out most of the food. Magdalena gave her a bowl of water, and because the monkey would not move, she lifted the bowl to her mouth, wetting her lips, spilling water down her chest. The monkey reached for her hand, and at first, Magdalena became frightened, thinking the monkey would bite her, but the monkey lay her hand on its belly and began picking imaginary lice from the back of Magdalena's hand.

This gesture made her smile, and with her other hand, Magdalena stroked the monkey's head. "You'll live then?" she said. "You'll survive."

For a long while Magdalena stared at the sea that gleamed like an immense flat sheet of iron under the brilliant sun. "I must," she murmured, "take care of myself."

The idea of renting out the cabaña had not occurred to her until her cousin Estrella mentioned that an American captain was looking for a place to rent. "Just for six months," Estrella said.

Magdalena thought about it and said, "Six months, no more."

Estrella and Nathan Spencer arrived one day when birds were building nests and Magdalena's German Shepherd was longing to join the other dogs outside the tall fence; and in the nearby sea, fish jumped up and caught the sun's rays. A picture-perfect day that gave the American captain the expression of one thoroughly enchanted.

"Asia is amazing," he said, while they sat in the living room. "In my short time here, I've seen how beautiful it is. I've seen rice paddies and forests, so green, like emerald, and stretching on forever. I've visited some temples and churches, both in Nam and here, and I can't get over the long and rich history of these places. Back home, we talk of 100-year-old buildings as old; over here people talk of thousands of years."

He was from Connecticut, twenty-five years old, tall and gawky. "From the air, everything looks lush and green, so I don't understand why Asian countries are poor. It's clear there are a lot of natural resources. The land is fertile; there are metal mines. There's coal. The place seems to have everything, so I don't get it," he said.

He loved the cabaña. "All this glass," he said, gesturing at the picture window and other windows, "it's so bright and I feel the sea is right at my doorstep." And he nodded approvingly at the Portuguese floor tiles with florid design; and he smiled at the indigo-and-white cushions and pillows on the white wicker furniture and the potted ferns, orchids, aloes and sword plants in the porcelain blue-and-white Chinese pots.

He moved into the cabaña but was rarely there so that Magdalena often forgot he was renting the place. Once, she brought the plumber to the cabaña to fix a leak, and she found a letter on the table. While waiting for the plumber, she could not resist reading it:

Dear Mom,

I received all your Christmas gifts, Anne's and Ravelle's included. Tell Anne the Hawaiian shirt is great. I've worn it several times and been mugged only once. Be sure and let her know the shirt really helps me blend in with the general populace out here. Tell Ravelle everyone over here loves the Dylan records but Chuck Berry is in demand. I've sent you some things, carved items and 'oa dais'; I hope you get them in time for Christmas.

Yes, it's true the air campaign has increased, but the plane I fly is the safest thing there is. I'm so far above the ground the SAMs can't reach me. The fighter planes are the ones getting it. For every two MiGs the Air Force gets, we lose one of our planes. Not the best kill-ratio. The navy's trying to do something about the situation; they've started their Top Gun school in San Diego; but the Air Force hasn't addressed the problem. Washington keeps assuring us the pilots of the MiGs are ignorant peasants poorly trained in Russia. One of them is Captain Nguyet Van Bay, a North Vietnamese pilot who claims seven kills. Not bad for an ignorant peasant, considering our ace is Colonel Robin Olds who has four North Vietnamese MiGs to his credit.

I'm saying all this lightly, but the situation is serious and has made me think a lot about why we're here and what we're doing here. Sometimes I feel as if I'm two people. There's the civilian Nathan who's asking what in hell he's doing here; and there's the captain who obeys orders and does his best. The captain must do his best. When I'm in the air, I can't muddle my brain with philosophical questions because people's lives depend on me. A millisecond is a long time when you're up there and need to think straight and react quickly. I can't afford to hem-and-haw when people's lives, including my own, are at stake. But in the silence of my room, I cannot help thinking.

I've seen and experienced much that has made me redefine democracy and wonder if the U.S. really is in this war for democracy. I look at South Vietnam and the puppet government we've propped up, and I realize that isn't much of a democracy. We're paying guys left and right to help us fight their war, and, to put it bluntly, they don't even like us.

In many ways, Dad's war was cut-and-dry. When Hitler went after the Jews and the Japanese bombed Pearl Harbor, well, matters were pretty clear. The bad guys were bad, the good guys, good. Even though lives were lost in that war as well, there was some sense and nobility to it all or at least one could pretend so. More and more I wish Dad were around so I could ask him about his war. I want to know if my thoughts and feelings jive with his. I want to know if he found himself walking around Asia as someone other than himself, that is, did he, as I find myself, become a symbol? Did people love him or hate him for no other reason than that he was an American? He never talked about killing anyone, but he must have. Did he see the person's face at all, and how did he feel? There's a lot of rhetoric about war, but the bottom line is, people are out there killing other people. It's not a pretty thought, nor is it a pretty sight, but it's really what war boils down to, after all the talk and politics and what-have-you.

I've been thinking about him a lot, remembering how he used to sit in his armchair in the living room, in the dark, with a glass of Scotch in his left hand and a smoldering cigarette in his right. I wonder now what it was all about, what all that sitting in the dark was about, what all that drinking was about, what all that pondering and obvious pain was about. It's funny how war can make you think.

I have many questions about my war, but no answers. I'm hoping the clowns in Washington do. They're playing politics out there, and we're simply trying to stay alive. It's like fighting with one hand tied behind your back. Needless to say, our morale is somewhat low.

I shouldn't be worrying you about these matters especially during Christmas. Despite what I've written, Asia hasn't been all that bad. I keep reminding myself that I'm stationed in one of the safest and friendliest bases over here. I've seen breathtaking places and met lovely people. But there's something about Christmas — it also makes you think, doesn't it? Christmas and those saccharin songs about the past and people you love. The memories and emotions bubble-up and there's no holding them back.

I miss all of you so terribly. And strangely, this seductive balmy weather makes me yearn for Colorado winters; I miss the dead silence when the snow *is falling at night and the blinding sight of the white, white snow in the morning. It's not going to be a white Christmas for us. After the monsoons passed, we've had sunny weather every day, around eighty degrees. I go swimming when I can in the sea that's as warm as bathwater — tell Anne to eat her heart out.*

Give my love to everyone, but keep most of it for yourself.

Your Son,
Nathan

After reading Nathan's letter, she carefully put it back, and she blushed.

She decided to pull up the rose garden, which had been Victor's idea in the first place. For days she worked side by side with the gardener in digging up the roses. One evening, Nathan stopped by to greet her. "The roses were dying," she explained, "They had always been sickly, no matter what we did. Constanzio was constantly fertilizing, but nothing helped. I grew tired of them. I'm going to put a pond here." And then as if to offer him something in return for the letter she had read, she said, "When I was a child, my father used to have a pond here. He put eight koi in it. And there were water lilies too. The whole thing was beautiful, unlike this." She swept her hand across the dug-up ground.

For a while she was lost in her thoughts then her brows furrowed: "The rose garden was a mistake. They were awful, dying sticks stuck in the middle of the garden, what a terrible sight that was. Like a nightmare. And I put up with it for years. How could I have allowed that?"

She shook her head, then her scowl vanished and her face lit up. "The fish were so tame, they used to stick their heads out of the water to beg for food. My father taught me how to pet their heads. Yes, you can stroke their heads. Most of the koi were orange, but one fish was orange and black. He was very large and friendly. After Papa died, my husband decided to get rid of the fishpond. We gave away all the koi except my favorite. We kept him in an enormous aquarium. I hand-fed him everyday, like I always did, but he died. He hated the aquarium. It was too small; there wasn't enough space for him to swim around. He was used to a large pond. He was a big fish, you see, with beautiful coloring, orange and black. His scales shimmered like mother of pearl. Do you like fish?"

Nathan nodded. "I had a goldfish. We kept him in a fish bowl on the kitchen window ledge. I won him at a school carnival. He lived for seven years."

"Goldfish don't live that long." Magdalena looked surprised and a bit amused.

"This one did. There's a story about him. We kept him in that bowl and fed him and changed his water now and then. He was just fine. One day I went out with a couple of friends in a truck. One of the kids had just turned sixteen and got his license. He was showing off, taking us out for a ride. We got into an accident. Two kids died, but I only had a small scratch on my leg. The strange thing is that the day that happened, my fish died for no reason at all. My mother always felt there was a connection between the accident and the fish dying."

"Yes, there is. The fish saved you," Magdalena said. "Things like that happen. If a pet dog or cat dies, we don't get too upset because we believe that the animal has taken the place of someone in the household. An exchange with Death — that is what we think. Did you have other fish?"

"Sure. After that fish died, I got another one. Now, this time I decided to take good care of this fish. I hadn't been cleaning the bowl of the first one all that well, and the water was always scummy. I decided to clean out the bowl every week with detergent. What I didn't know was that soap kills fish. The second fish died right away. I got another one, and that one died as well. It took me a while to figure out the problem, but by that time, my mother had grown tired of the whole thing and had given the bowl away."

Magdalena laughed. It was the first time he had seen her laugh, and the sound of her voice lingered in his mind even as he flew over blue seas and green paddies. He decided to give her an orange and black koi for her new pond. After a lot of checking he found a private collector in Saigon, and he selected a fish that moved briskly. When her pond was completed, he presented this to her. The fish, about half-a-foot long, was swimming in a bucket of water.

He had rehearsed what he would say to her, shuffling words back and forth in his head, running the scene over and over of where they would be when he'd give her the fish, what she would look like, how she would react, but in the end he said simply, "I don't know what your fish looked like, but this is for you." He placed the bucket in front of her.

They were near the pond. The crickets were buzzing loudly and the waves of the sea beyond had settled into gentle lapping. Constanzio had built a small bonfire of branches and dry leaves that he had carefully swept under the fruit-bearing trees, and ribbons of gray smoke trickled upward from the smoldering fire.

She got down on her knees to study the fish. She put her hand in the water and with one finger gently touched the back of the fish. "He didn't look exactly like this, but this is a pretty fish. Look at his scales, how brilliant his colors are. He's a beautiful fish." She picked up the bucket and carefully released the fish into the water. Quickly the fish hid under some water lilies. She picked up a stone and tapped the side of the pond.

"What was the name of your fish? The one that died?" She was still on her knees.

He paused, "I'm afraid I gave him the very unimaginative name of Goldie."

"Goldie," she repeated, and wrinkled her nose in disapproval. "All right, I'll name this one Goldie."

The fish darted out from its hiding place and Magdalena took a quick breath. She watched the fish swim in circles. She tapped the rock on the side of the pond again. "This is how you call them," she explained, and she felt a contentment she had not felt in a long time.

Her scent used to arouse Victor; the rustling of her skirt made him cast lustful glances at her. He was always touching her, stroking her hair, massaging the back of her neck. His attention made her love him in the first place. He made her feel important, special, beautiful. In a way, his desire for her made her feel powerful. During supper at her parents' home, he slipped his hand under her skirt and touched her, making her bite her lower lip and blush. Her mother, unaware of what was happening said, "Be careful of the shrimps, Magdalena, you look like you're having an allergic reaction." Victor was always suggesting new ways of lovemaking, different ways, ways the nuns at St. Catherine's had not even warned her about. "That's strange Victor," she used to say. Well, Victor was gone and she was left with the monkey farm, this house, her life.

Alone in her bedroom, with doors locked, she stared at herself in the armoire mirror. How strange her body appeared. So pale, with curves she hardly knew. It had been a long time since she looked at herself. She never thought much of her body. She was always so busy; her body was just there. At school, the nuns gave her the idea that her body was sinful — if she ate too much, that was gluttony, if she enjoyed too much, that was excess. Breasts, buttocks, thighs, and legs had to be covered, must not be revealed. Sister Damiana had even taught her how to dress and undress without exposing her body. Victor was the exact opposite; he wanted her to show her body. He brought home ridiculous nightgowns; he wanted her to be someone she was not. He treated her body as if it were a plaything. And like a petulant child, he grew tired with this toy.

She touched her breasts, her stomach, her neck, her thighs, the back of her legs, the area between her legs. One day soon, this body will be old; and not too long afterwards, it will turn into dust. This thought frightened her, made her think how insignificant she was, made her realize that she alone gave her life significance.

It was almost sunset and from the verandah of the main house she watched Nathan Spencer strolling on the seashore. He was heading towards the end of the bay. Occasionally he bent over to pick a flat stone, which he threw into the water. He was making them skip; she had walked with him and watched him count the number of jumps the stones made. It amazed her to see a grown man behave like a child. Like a boy he talked to her about his father who used to sit in the dark living room, smoking cigarettes and drinking Scotch, and he wondering, wondering all the time what that meant. One evening as they watched the moon sailing over the tranquil bay, he told her about Vietnam, how green it was, and how sad. Earlier this afternoon, he stopped by to give her a conch shell that he had found on the other side of the island. "Have you ever seen one like this? This is perfect."

He was a little bit in love with her, this man-boy. For weeks now he had been following her around, finding every excuse to see her, to talk to her. She thought that she could go to him one night, in the dark when the servants were asleep. No one would know as she slipped into the cabaña, into his room, and lay on the bed beside him. Then maybe she could get even with Victor — an act of infidelity against a thousand.

For all the times Victor called her Mother Superior, she would kiss this man with her mouth open; for all the times Victor said she was not free sexually, she would lick his body; for all the times Victor made love to other women, she would mount him, take him in, lead them both to destruction or salvation — she did not know which.

A memory came to her. She and Victor alone one afternoon. They had been swimming in the sea. It was April and hot, and the water cooled their bodies. She floated on her back, feeling the sea rock her to and fro, feeling contented. Victor dove under her and tickled her back. Startled, she lost her balance and sputtered about. Victor held her, pushed her hair back and began kissing her.

"Victor," she said, in a reprimanding voice.

"Magdalena," he countered, licking the salt water off her neck. He tried to slip off her bathing suit.

"Not here Victor."

He stopped, grabbed her hand and pulled her ashore, toward the cabaña. "Come on, then. I've always wanted to do it in your parents' room."

He brought her to the bedroom and pushed her unto the bed.

"Victor, stop it." Her heart was pounding, blood rushing to every part of her body.

He removed her bathing suit and began kissing her breasts. Later, he began kissing her stomach. His movements grew more frenetic, and when his mouth traveled downward, she knew what he had in mind. She quickly crossed her legs and tried to push him off. "No!"

"Why not?" he cajoled.

"Because."

He resumed kissing her belly button until she relaxed, until the pit of her stomach quickened. She bit her lower lip, trying to maintain control. Then when he had kissed her in a way that made her arch her back, he quickly pushed her legs apart. He lowered his head and kissed her there, did things to her, so that her hand flew to the back of his head, and she held him down, guided him while she panted and gasped for air like one drowning. Very quickly, Victor changed his position so his thighs were near her head. She, following some primal instinct, reached, took Victor into her mouth, and like an echo, followed his lead. Even while this was happening, she thought of pulling away, but her mouth, strong yet soft, moved on its own. She struggled but it was hopeless. She found herself sliding, sliding into some dark swirling pool and her stomach quivered and relaxed and her soul exploded from that pool up to the stars. She was gone. For a fraction of time, she was nowhere.

It was wonderful.

And frightening.

She hated the feeling of totally losing herself. She feared the sensation of losing touch with reality, of disappearing into the heavens, of being one with Victor.

It came to her that her body was some kind of machine. It could do things against her volition — that was what was frightening. It could respond to hunger, to fear, to anger, to sex, and she, Magdalena Sotelo, could not stop it, could not control it. It was frightening.

Standing there, staring at the dying sun, she realized that ever since that lovemaking incident with Victor, she never allowed herself to be as totally lost ever again. It was as if she'd locked a part of herself, locked it in a vault and flung it into the deepest part of the sea, and she would never lose control in that way again. Standing there, she thought that it was a good thing, a very wise thing that she held part of herself back from Victor. And it was just as well, she thought, because now Victor was gone.

Nathan Spencer returned to the cabaña. He opened the front door. She could see his gangly motions as he pulled a chair and sat by the doorway. He picked up a guitar and started strumming. He sang and the words of his folk songs drifted into the verandah — words of war and peace, of love and sadness, of life and death.

And as she watched and listened to him, the thought took shape in her head: Maybe tonight, I will go to him.

The Cabaña

Magdalena lived in a seafront property in the small island of Mactan, a channel across from Ubec Island. Her father Fermin Sanchez's family had owned it for so long, no one remembered exactly how his family acquired it. Family legend referred to a widow whose son had killed a Spanish official over some woman. Before the authorities caught him, the mother sold the property to Fermin's great-great-grandfather and she quickly placed her son on a galleon headed for Acapulco.

Another story claimed that the hero Lapu-Lapu, who slayed the Portuguese navigator Ferdinand Magellan, had grown up on that land, that it was the gut-wrenching beauty of the place that had shaped the boy into a fierce nationalist.

There was talk that the property had a hidden tunnel connecting Mactan Island to Ubec Island, that during times of war, ancient kings used this tunnel to flee enemies or hide their wealth.

The land was rocky but riddled with coconut trees, hibiscus, birds of paradise and a colorful profusion of tropical bushes. It curved around a cove with calm blue sea and sugary white sand; and even the people of Ubec who were not fond of swimming in the sea nor of sunbathing, acknowledged that it was a prime piece of property.

Fermin Sanchez loved sea-air and water. Long before seaside resorts became popular, when women cowered under umbrellas to protect their skin from the fierce sun, he built a house on that property. A lover of nature, Fermin created a house that followed the contour of the land and curved around trees he did not have the heart to chop down. Glass windows and glass doors insured a magnificent view of the sand and sea from every room, even the bathroom with the sunken bathtub.

The Mactan property served as the family vacation house. Weekends, the Sanchez family would pile into the station wagon, take the barge across the channel, and go to the beach house. There they barbecued fish so fresh it was still squirming when the cook gutted it. They swam and picked shells and poked around tide-pools teeming with starfish, sea cucumbers, mussels, and other sea creatures. At night, they marveled at the brilliance of the moon and stars and the rhythmic lapping of the waves on the sand and the salty breeze that lulled them to peaceful sleep.

When Magdalena married Victor, her father gave her the house and property, making sure it was recorded in Fermin's and Magdalena's names, and not in Victor's name for fear Victor would claim the land. When Magdalena and Victor settled in the main house, Fermin and Luisa built the cabaña for their own use.

The cabaña was a separate wing with a bedroom, bathroom, living room, kitchen, and dining room. Like the main house, it was full of glass and was so light and airy, visitors claimed they felt they could float out to the sea.

Magdalena's parents decorated the cabaña as if it were their special playhouse. They ordered Portuguese floor tiles with an elaborate floral design. Luisa hired a seamstress to sew indigo and white cushions and pillows for the white wicker furniture. She personally potted ferns, orchids, aloes, and fortune plants in porcelain blue-and-white Chinese pots. The shelves against the walls displayed Luisa's antique statues and Fermin's ancient masks from distant regions. And outside, Fermin built a pond which he stocked with colorful koi, fish so tame they ate from their hands, that is until Victor decided to replace the pond with a rose garden instead, roses that grew up gnarled and ugly, and paradise in this land became a word, not a reality.

Winning Hearts and Minds(1967)

During a visit to Nakhon Panom Air Base in Thailand, Colonel March Adams heard that Major Ron O'Connor had been shot down during a strike near the Plain of Jars, in Laos. When he returned to Mactan Air Force Base, which he commanded, he told his men about O'Connor, how he had been a member of the reputed 602nd Special Operations Squadron, which was primarily a search-and-rescue (SAR) outfit, responsible for all of Laos and parts of Cambodia. Known as the Sandy Mission, the 602nd also conducted strikes in Northern Laos and made sorties against the Vietcong enemy truck and troop convoys along Ho Chi Minh Trail; but they were famous for their rescue efforts. O'Connor and his wingman, Captain Jose Cass, had been on a rescue mission to save a gunned-down pilot when the enemy got their plane. The pilot whom they had tried to save in the first place, survived; but Major O'Connor "bought the farm," as the colonel called it.

He said this matter-of-factly. This was his second war, and he had learned to look at war in terms of wins and losses, as if it were a giant chess game with pawns and horses sacrificed for the more important chess pieces.

His men, however, were young, and they assumed a somber tone. "I knew Ron," someone said, "he's got a wife and two kids."

Another spoke: "Once I went with Ron to Francois Restaurant. He had heard that Francois was the best French restaurant in Vietnam. Only problem was, Francois was in VC territory. No problem, Ron said, the VC left Francois' clients alone. So one Friday, a group of us went, three jeeps, and guys holding machine guns all the way through VC territory to Francois. We picked a table that backed up against a wall and guys continued taking turns with the machine guns throughout the entire meal. We ate and had a lot of laughs. Oh, man, I can't believe he's gone."

Thinking to console them, the colonel added, "His commanding officer recommended he be listed as MIA (missing in action) instead of KIA-NBR (killed in action, no body recovered) so his widow will continue collecting twenty grand a year. If he's KIA-NBR, she'll get a lump-sum settlement and less than half the continued compensation."

The airmen proceeded to talk about their preferred listing if something did happen to them in Southeast Asia. Some men agreed that MIA was a better deal for their families; others thought the psychological anguish would be torture on them. The overall tone of the conversation turned so grim that all of them jumped at the suggestion to go to St. Moritz Bar.

The owner of the bar was an expatriate German named Karl, a loud, effusive man, whose life centered on his bar. "We have some new girls," Karl said with a thick German accent. He gestured toward the stage in the center of the bar where half a dozen Go-Go girls were dancing. "Some clubs have goldfish, I have beautiful girls." He sat beside the colonel and ordered a bottle of Scotch for the Americans. "Look at that. Just look at that, their bikinis are no larger than postage stamps," he said with a wink.

The airmen laughed and hooted. The colonel relaxed, glad that the fiery memory of O'Connor was receding from his men's minds.

"They come to me, begging for work," Karl continued. "I take good care of them. Why, some of them have married my clients! Last month, a dancer stopped by with her New Yorker husband — and a three-carat diamond ring. Not too bad for someone from a barrio. I am the one who picks them, each and everyone of them. I go to small barrios; I pick the prettiest. Sometimes I pick some ugly ones, like that one over there who looks like King Kong. Believe it or not, some men like ugly girls. But this girl with the ring, she was beautiful. And obedient. What else can a man want? Her husband must be very happy." He slapped his thigh and guffawed.

The colonel glanced at the smiling dancers who were furiously gyrating; and for some reason, he remembered his wife, two children, and their Golden Retriever back in Charleston, South Carolina. It had been five months since he met his wife in Honolulu for a brief R&R; and he wondered how she was.

"So, Colonel, how is your war coming along? News is always about Vietnam. Last week there was a picture in *Time* of a village burning. And inside, a story about more American bombings. The North, the South, they don't get along. It is a mess, ja? Well, here in St. Moritz, everybody get along. Have more whiskey, Colonel."

Before the colonel could answer, the German left. The colonel was relieved. The German's accent grated on his nerves, bringing back memories of an earlier war.

The whiskey loosened the knots in his shoulders. He closed his eyes and pictured the airy houses in Charleston. He imagined himself walking along the city walls, looking across the sea at Fort Sumter. He recalled his grade school teacher, Miss Hill, a passionate Southerner, proudly relate the story of how Charlestonians had bombarded the fort, thus starting the Civil War. As a little boy, he used to recreate famous battles like the Battle of Gettysburg, using small toy metal soldiers. He wondered what happened to the toy soldiers. The last time he had seen them, they were in a box in his mother's attic.

A girl spoke, startling him. "Maybe you find it one day."

He raised an eyebrow at the girl who had sat beside him.

"What you are looking for," she continued. "A while ago, you said, 'I need to find them.'"

Embarrassed that he had voiced his foolish thoughts, he said, "It was nothing."

"Do you want more Scotch? Sir says to take care of you." She pointed at the German who was now at the other end of the room.

"I'm sorry, I have to leave."

"If you go, he'll think I'm no good. He's watching me because I'm new here. I'm a singer. I started work last Wednesday. Were you here last week?" she asked.

The colonel shook his head. "No, I was in Pleiku."

"What's 'Pleiku'? A beach or something?"

"No, not a beach."

"Here in Philippines? Or someplace else?"

"In Vietnam," he said, irritated at her persistence.

"Ah, yes, Vietnam. Is there fighting in Pleiku?"

"It's a place in Vietnam, that's all." He didn't add that driving toward Pleiku, he had seen graves on either side of the highway. Markers, as far as the eyes could see, 150,000 of them, an endless stretch of worn, gray-white markers. An ocean of grave markers. Thousands of these were graves of French soldiers who had died at Dien Bien Phu. For the rest of his life, he would never forget the sight of those markers.

"You have to be happy like others. Sir likes everyone happy. Want to dance?" She gestured toward the pulsating dance floor.

The colonel shook his head.

She hesitated, but said: "Maybe you want a good time? Bar-fee is twenty dollars, but the boss says to go with you, no problem. He wants you to have a good time. He likes Americans here. Lots of dollars. I can give you a good time. Two hours, three hours, even four, forget the sad times; be happy. But not all night. I go home before morning."

She was wearing tight black pants and a sparkly red top. Although her lips were bright red, her face looked young, like a fourteen-year-old playing grownup. Her hand was resting near his, and her skin looked soft. For a moment, the colonel imagined the feel of human skin against his, and how comforting that would be; and he was tempted. No one would care; and his wife wouldn't know. He could take her to the hotel down the street; they could be together for a couple of hours. He would feel her body, taste her lips, find release; he would forget O'Connor, Pleiku, the war. One-hundred-twenty-minutes, that was all; and there the matter would end.

But quickly lust gave way to anger at his weakness; and later, anger at the corruptness in Asia, how women like their politicians sold themselves, just like that. Here there was a price for everything. And here, in this far-off, God-forsaken place, men like O'Connor were dying. What for? What were they sacrificing their lives for? If he died, would he have died for his country, or for Asia? And what in hell were they doing in Asia in the first place, a place he didn't even like, peopled by people he couldn't even understand; peopled by people who didn't even like Americans? What was it all about? Americans would bleed to death as the French had in Dien Bien Phu until it fell in 1954. That was the fate of Americans in Vietnam. This war was a waste of time, a waste of money, a waste of American lives.

He got up, ramrod, and headed for the door.

Unfazed, the girl shouted after him, "I'll tell sir you have a wife back home."

Saturday, the colonel did a double-take when Captain Nathan Spencer reminded him about his afternoon schedule.

"A child care what?" the colonel shouted.

"Its inauguration, sir. A child care center, in Ubec. You'd okayed giving them old medical and dental equipment, Colonel, and the women had invited you to give a talk. You said yes."

"I don't care about the equipment; they've had it. But what is this about a talk? I'm here to fight a war, not to give goddamn lectures."

"You accepted their invitation, Colonel, sir. You agreed it may be a good way to win the hearts and minds of the people. I understand the center is for children of prostitutes, Colonel, and apparently a lot of the kids are half-Americans. The women organizing the event wanted to make sure you're aware the archbishop and mayor will be speaking along with you, Colonel."

"The church and state will be there, so by gum, the US government must be represented."

"Something like that, Colonel."

"Well, then, you come along, Captain."

Before serving in Asia, Colonel Adams had been part of the mission at the North American Air Defense Command in Colorado and he had taught part-time at the Air Force Academy in Colorado Springs where he had met Captain Nathan Spencer and struck a friendship with him. He liked the young man and gave him what he considered fatherly advice.

On the way to the city, the captain said, "I can't help wondering, Colonel, about the poverty here. I understand there are a lot of resources, gold, silver, copper; the land is rich. I've flown over acres and acres of green rice paddies; clearly the land is fertile. Yet I've heard babies die from disease and hunger. It's fascinating, Colonel, the contrast between the beauty and poverty here. I can't figure it out."

"Corruption, Spencer. There's corruption in every level of society. You can't get anything done without paying someone. We're doing our best for them, trying to establish a democracy in these countries, but sometimes I wonder if it's worth it."

"And there's the question of democracy, Colonel. I've read the Vietnamese government is repressive. And we're supporting them, Sir. I should be simply doing my job, I know that Colonel; but I saw that picture in *Time*, a Vietnamese village, sir, in flames, with a child bleeding, and other people around. And Colonel, well, when we're up in the air, we don't see the faces of these people. The navigator locates the target; the bombardier pushes the button; and we return to the base. I guess what I'm saying Colonel, was that it felt strange to see that picture, to realize we were responsible for all that."

"Let me give you sound advice, Captain. Don't do drugs; avoid the women; do your job in the best way you can, and you'll get out of here alive." It had sounded so simple; surely Ron O'Connor had followed that advice, but Ron was dead. The colonel wondered what else was needed to survive this war.

Erlinda Sabados and Josie Martinez, president and vice-president respectively of the Catholic Women of the Virgin Mary Most Pure, greeted the men. "Colonel Adams, Captain Spencer," Erlinda began in a sing-song voice, "how nice of you to join us. We are happy, so very happy that you are here with us." She was a large woman, a spinster, in her mid-fifties.

"So happy, Colonel," said Josie who was a younger, smaller version of Erlinda (Erlinda's shadow, Ubecans called her).

"You have fifteen minutes, Colonel. You come after Archbishop Montalban and the mayor. You're with two very important figures in Ubec, so you see Colonel, how much we consider American support an honor." Erlinda stood on tiptoe and draped a sampaguita lei over Colonel Adam's neck and another over Captain Spencer's neck.

"An honor," Josie echoed.

"Some GROs will be present Colonel. The women. The mothers of the unfortunate children. Out of *delicadeza*, we call them GROs," Erlinda whispered.

"Guest Relation Officers," explained Josie.

"Even before Kaugma-an was finished, twenty children signed up, Colonel. Somehow, the GROs heard about the center and begged that we take their children in. Because they are out all night, they sleep in the daytime, leaving the children totally unattended. No Catholic training whatsoever, none. Those poor children grow up like heathens. A place like this is a haven to them. The GROs have been particularly busy, Colonel, as you know. Since you Americans expanded your base, there are quite a lot of soldiers around our city.

"I'll be frank, Colonel, when I first introduced the idea of a child care center, there was great resistance from members. They accused me of avoiding the real issue, prostitution. They insisted prostitution is immoral, corrupt, not to mention unhealthy; and that prostitution needs to be stopped once and for all. I agreed with them; but the question was how to stop prostitution. How do you stop the oldest profession? Do you have the answer, Colonel? I didn't. We thought that since GROs were in the business for money, we could start a training center to teach them some other trade — sewing perhaps, or cooking, or some other small cottage industry. The idea was shot down by a GRO herself who said it would take a week of stitching rag-dolls to earn what she made in one night as a prostitute. And of course your base, these Americans on R&R with their dollars to spend — well, it was an issue of economics, pure and simple, and eventually the others supported my proposed child care center project, hoping to save these children since we can do nothing more for the mothers."

This was a matter that the colonel had never even remotely

considered, and he became curious. He asked if the center's name, Kaugma-an, meant anything; and he nodded approvingly when Erlinda said it meant tomorrow. He observed the three rooms that served as classrooms, the kitchen, the nursery, and the clinic with the American equipment. He was glad that he had had the wisdom to give them the old equipment.

The women led them to some chairs near the podium in one of the larger classrooms, and they left to test the mike and gather everyone for the program.

The mayor and archbishop, who were already seated, were discussing the Catholic Women.

"These women are the backbone of Ubec society," the archbishop expounded. "Good and pure. They do not let their wealth get in their way. They see everything in clear perspective. They fixed up the old Spanish fort; now they are taking care of these unfortunate children. They use their own money; they beg, they borrow, they virtually steal, to get these worthy projects done. But they get them done. God bless them."

The mayor spoke: "Your Imminence, let's not forget the city donated the building. It's old, that's true, but it's rent-free. And of course Your Excellency, our good American friends here have donated medical and dental equipment. You cannot imagine, Colonel, how very much appreciated these things are. The doctors, all volunteers by the way, had nothing more than stethoscopes — I exaggerate — but seriously, they had little else. But now, they have these fancy American equipment, why these are better than the equipment at Ubec General Hospital."

The colonel felt embarrassed; he had simply been junking the equipment. Helping these children, these people, had been the last thing in his mind.

Erlinda and Josie returned with soft drinks and plates of food, which they set in a low table in front of the men, and then Erlinda started the program.

She spoke for a long time, and the solitary electric fan could not dispel the heat that sprang from the cement floor. The colonel took his handkerchief from his pocket and mopped his brow. He glanced at his watch, and noted that it was already mid-afternoon. Tomorrow, he would have to fly to Vietnam for a meeting with General Westmoreland.

The program plodded along.

Erlinda introduced another member of the Catholic Women, who in turn introduced a priest, who in turn introduced Archbishop Montalban. The archbishop congratulated the Catholic Women on the completion of the child care center; he praised their vision in responding to "what was happening in Ubec in the face of the expansion of the nearby military facility." He touched, very delicately, on the unfortunate reality that GROs could not afford to acquire respectable jobs; and he talked at great length about the children of these women, the innocent children, who fortunately would be in a proper Catholic environment within this child care center.

Erlinda returned to introduce the mayor who kicked off his talk by reading an excerpt from "The Hound of Heaven." Nobody got the connection between the poem and the center, but the mayor was an eloquent orator, and he segued nicely into a detailed account of how the Catholic Women had asked him for the city's support, how delighted he had been that he could provide assistance, and he assured everyone he would continue to help them as long as he remained in office.

It was the colonel's turn. Erlinda introduced him. Colonel Adams had planned on speaking for no more than five minutes. He surprised himself when words flowed. He side-stepped the issue of prostitution and the question of the children's paternity and started to talk about how pleased the American people were to provide assistance to Filipinos and other Asians. He found himself elaborating on how Americans wanted nothing better than to win the hearts and minds of the people. When he sat down, he thought he had sounded more like a USAID officer than an Air Force Colonel. He felt embarrassed.

There were more speeches from various officers of the Catholic Women, from the doctors who volunteered at the clinic, from the woman who made lunches and snacks, from the restaurateur who donated food, and then, to the colonel's great surprise, a familiar-looking woman took the mike. It was the singer at St. Moritz Bar. The memory flustered him. He hoped she would not recognize him.

Her eyes paused ever slightly at the Colonel, but her face showed no sign of recognition. "Good afternoon, ladies and gentlemen. I am a singer," she began, "I sing at night, at St. Moritz. Some people say it is a bad place, but they pay and I am able to buy food and clothes for my child. I have a little boy. At night he is with my mother, but in the daytime, he comes here. He can now make the Sign of the Cross; and he can say 'Jesus.' One day he will have a better life than me; and it will be because of you. Kaugma-an — Tomorrow — he will do better than me. Thank you. Now I will sing."

She sang a plaintive rendition of "We Shall Overcome" followed by a rowdier "Boots Were Made for Walking." A ripple of tension swept through the audience when the singer marched provocatively around the room, but vanished when the archbishop himself cocked his head to one side, and started snapping his fingers in time to the music.

Later, the singer brought the children to the middle of the room. The older children giggled and pushed one another. The younger children clung to the woman's legs. The colonel wondered which one was her son. When they were in position, the woman whispered something to the children that made them smile and relax. Eyes riveted on them, she lifted a finger and led the children to sing a playful Ubecan song about a local fisherman, Filemon, catching a *tambasakan* fish. After, they sang a couple of medleys that involved audience participation.

There was a final dance number by the younger members of the Catholic Women who did a bamboo dance. Clad in colorful native costume, they hopped and glided over bamboo poles that were rhythmically banged together; and finally the program ended.

Colonel Adams and Captain Spencer got up and said goodbye to the mayor and the archbishop, who suddenly exclaimed to people's bewilderment, "Yes, Sinatra! The daughter sang the song!"

Erlinda and Josie escorted them to the main door. There, waiting by the side was the singer, with a little boy in her arms.

"Sir," she called, addressing the colonel, to the surprise of everyone. They paused. "This is my son," she continued.

The colonel looked at the child.

"I come home to him every night, after work. Every night without fail," the singer said.

"He's a nice-looking boy."

"Do you think so? Sometimes he is naughty."

"A strong will, that is all. He has strong jaws. A strong will is good."

"I want him to do better than me."

"I believe he will. He'll do all right."

The singer beamed. "Thank you, sir. Goodbye."

The colonel nodded and he and the captain continued to the

doorway. They said goodbye to Erlinda and Josie who appeared puzzled at the exchange.

When they were in their car, the captain said, "That was a good speech, Colonel."

"I overdid it, Captain. I'm a soldier, not anything else."

"Oh, no, Colonel, I believe your speech won their hearts and minds."

The colonel looked out the window and saw shanties along the road and piles of garbage. Young children, no older than the bigger children at the child care center, were rummaging through the garbage. Sticks in their hands, they poked through incredible filth to find empty bottles and newspapers, little treasures which they could later sell. He must have seen them before; but this was the first time the colonel noticed these children. How peculiar Asia was, he thought, with all its different facets.

He paused and said, "And I'm afraid, Captain, they have won ours."

Magdalena's Monologue
(1967)

He tastes of the sea this man. He is like a god risen from the sea. I like to cup his face in my palms, touch his neck, his arm, feel his skin against mine. He is always warm, warmer than me: he says it is from desire. In the semi-darkness, I stand against him and lick his neck — first the one side, then the other. The smoothness of his skin, that slight salty taste amazes me. Sometimes I bite him gently, and I leave lovemarks on his chest and neck, as if to brand him. He tries to do the same, but I shake my head. A part of me fears Victor may return and find those marks, and know what I've done.

I am unfaithful and so we do not speak. It is as if we are other people in another place. In the beginning, he would talk and tell me how beautiful I am, how desirable. But his words would jar me, make thoughts flow through my mind, and I knew I did not belong in that cabaña with him, that I should leave, and I was filled with great confusion. It is better when we are silent. The moment I enter his room and close the door, we do not exchange a word. There is always something frightening when I lock that door. It is forbidden. I hold my breath, but my heart pounds. I fear someone will barge in — the servants, or Victor himself. After the metallic click of the latch, we hear only the crickets outside and the rhythmic pounding sea. I place my finger on his lips to silence him. He kisses my fingertips, my hand, my arm, my neck. It is as if he and I are riding an enormous wave. Every cell of our bodies awakens and we can feel the coolness of the breeze, the warmth of the other. We melt, he and I, in a sea of desire that laps back and forth, this enormous ocean on which we flounder, working hard to satisfy that desire, end that palpable, palpitating wanting. Fingers touching, lips kissing, tongues probing. Once, in the semi-darkness I saw sparks from our fingers when they touched. Could that be so? I wanted to ask but could not break our unspoken promise of silence. We float, he and I, on this wave of desire, rising higher and higher. Sometimes to torture him, I pull away and walk around the room naked, knowing he is desiring me. And once, when the moon was full and moonlight streamed into a window, I stood by the window so the rays fell on my breasts, the curve of my neck, my waist, my sex, and I knew I glowed like some moon goddess. He from the sea, I from the moon.

He likes to watch me. From the moment I enter, he observes me, noticing everything about me, a new hairdo, new nailpolish, a little scratch on my arm. He likes to see me desire him. This is what he sometimes does: he kisses me, his mouth sucking my lower lip, and when I kiss back, he pulls away to look at me. My face is tilted upward, eyes closed, lost in the sensation of his soft mouth on mine. When I open my eyes slowly, as if waking from some wonderful dream, he is staring at me, then he kisses me again. This time he runs his tongue into my mouth, and just when I start to suck his tongue, he pulls away again just to watch me, as if watching me is pleasurable as well. He does this several times, until I feel I am going mad, then he pulls me up and holds me tight so I can feel his body, feel his hardness. I think surely he will take me now. But he walks back into the shadows while I stand in the middle of the room, expectant, full of desire, until I approach him and touch his hardness, pull him towards me. And then comes the breathing and skin rubbing skin, and moisture and sweat and the rhythmic sounds of the bed rocking. Those are the only sounds.

On the beach, away from our sanctuary of silence, he asked me about the first time I made love. I shouldn't have but I told him anyway. It was with Victor, after a party, and we had driven up to the hills. There he had kissed my mouth and touched my breasts, and kissed my nipples, then he slid his hand under my skirt and began touching me there until I grew moist and lost all sense of time, of place, of decency. We tried to do it there, but Victor had a difficult time. I was too tight. He said we'd go someplace private; and so we went to Stardust Motel, drove into a garage and walked up a room. I did not know what to expect, and I was frightened. I told Victor this, and he kissed my hand and said we didn't have to do anything, we could just talk if that was what I wanted. I felt safer, more relaxed. We sat side by side on the bed for a while, my head resting on his shoulder, he stroking my hair. Then he started kissing me once again and touching me, gently, softly, always pulling back when I became agitated. When he started kissing my breasts through my blouse, I didn't even realize that I was the one who unbuttoned my top. I wanted him that much. He repeated that we didn't have to do it, that his rubbing against me would feel good. We were now in bed, without any clothes on. He was on top of me; instead of touching me there with his hand, he used his manhood — rubbing me there back and forth in a rhythm that was mesmerizing. Suddenly I felt a sharp sensation of pleasure; it happened when he rubbed me in a certain place; and he did this over and over until my breathing grew rapid and my body quivered. "You came," he said. I didn't know what that meant, I only knew I wanted him to enter me. It was difficult and there was much pain and blood. But later, when he entered me again, it was better. Victor was a good lover; he knew how to wait until I was the one begging him to do things to me.

I did not tell him everything but my sea god became jealous. He walked toward the sea and threw a stone into the water. He stood there for a long time, studying the bay. Then he turned to me. "You love him," he said.

"I *loved* him. I married him," I said, as if that absolved everything.

"How can you continue to love him after all he's done to you?"

"I said 'I loved him.' I was young then. I am no longer so young."

Still my sea-god remained distant until I went to him and stroked his hair and caressed his cheek, and he kissed the palm of my hand, and I felt his warm breath.

"I love you," he said, and the most frightening thought entered my mind: I could love this man.

Estrella Finds God in a Hospital Room

He'd been calling me all along, but I didn't listen. He'd called me that Christmas Eve when Esteban didn't go to church with me, and I had to go alone with *Tiya* Luisa and Magdalena. In Guadalupe Church, we found seats in front near the giant nativity set, which was decorated with red poinsettias and twinkling lights that Father Ybanez had picked up on sale at the White Gold House. I saw four children abandon their parents to take a close look at the giant figure of the Baby Jesus. Before that night, only the figurines of Joseph, Mary, the Three Kings, some shepherds and a seraphic angel dangling from the ceiling, had populated the nativity set. The children pointed at the Infant Jesus; they were giggling with excitement; their little faces shone. I remembered how Magdalena and I had done the same thing when we were children, how we had driven ourselves breathless with excitement, our childish anticipation had been boundless. Giddy for weeks before, during, and after Christmas, we didn't wind down until the feast day of the Three Kings.

That night, when God called me, I had watched the children bubble with life and I realized I had no life in me. I was cold, unmoving. I was no better than the cold, expressionless statues scattered around the church. I looked at the people around me, their lips stretched into broad smiles, their faces lit up with joy, while I went through the motions of kneeling, standing, sitting, mouthing my prayers, without feeling anything. Nothing — I felt nothing. I was a mechanical doll, lethargic, not caring one whit that after Mass I'd proceed to my aunt's house to celebrate the *noche buena* meal, that tomorrow I'd have lunch at Magdalena's house, that in a few days it'd be Holy Innocents, and that the new New Year was around the corner. God's call came in the form of the arduous days that stretched in front me, strung together in a colorless, bland way, an infinity of waking up in the morning, dragging around during the daytime, and tossing and turning in bed at night.

But I didn't listen.

What made me deaf was my love for Esteban. From the start I was crazy about him. I broke all rules of society and God because of him. I was shameless; I was a sinner. I should have been named Magdalena, instead of Estrella the Star. I was the Mary Magdalene.

Listen:

When I was only seventeen, Esteban stirred my flesh, turned me shameless, taught me about lust.

A very long time ago, long before I found God — praise Him who had the infinite patience to wait for me to come around — Esteban and I had been slow-dancing. I remember it well. It was at Magdalena's party. He had run his hand up and down my back to feel the snaps of my bra. I tried to maintain a decent distance but Esteban pulled me close to him and his warm breath blew gently against my ear and neck, so warm like a humid summer day, and my stomach fluttered. Song after song floated by, and Esteban's breath became short and labored until he pulled away and whispered in that liquid-gold voice of his, "Let's go."

"Where?" I had asked, innocently.

"Out. It's too hot in here. Let's go for a ride."

I told Magdalena I was leaving, that Esteban would take me home. She had given me a look and I had laughed softly and murmured, "I have a headache and want to go home."

Esteban and I walked to the car casually, as if indeed he was merely driving me home. He didn't even hold my hand or put his arm around me. In the car, I sat close to the door so people watching could see the great distance between us.

Like Satan, he knew precisely which words to use to catch his prey. He broke the awkward silence. "They should have opened the windows."

"Some of the windows were jammed, but sure they should have opened the doors."

"The verandah doors were open, but there was no breeze. It's May," he said.

"Cantaloupes will be out soon. I love cantaloupes," I said.

"Do you?"

"Especially melon balls with lots of sugar," I continued. "It's the juice I love, especially on a hot day. It's so much better than Coke. It's like an explosion in your mouth. So sweet and cool."

Esteban chuckled.

"What's funny?"

"You," he said. "Come here."

I became shy and turned my body so I was looking straight ahead.

"Don't move away, come here," Esteban repeated.

I slid over, but just a little bit so a respectable distance remained between us.

By now we were going up the hill and the crickets grew louder and the cool breeze felt good. On top of the hill, away from civilization, Esteban parked and turned off the headlights. For a brief while darkness engulfed us, but soon we could see the flickering city lights below, and above us the stars and a crescent moon. Esteban shifted his weight. He leaned back and straightened his legs out toward the passenger side so his shoes touched my legs. I moved my legs away. Clinging to the door handle, I peered up at the stars. "Look at all those stars," I said, hoping to clear the growing tension in the car. "I've never seen so many. Let's find a shooting star, so we can make a wish."

Laughing, Esteban took my hand in his and kissed my palm. Then he kissed my fingers, except my right pinkie, which he put into his mouth. "I feel like eating you all up," he said. He gently clamped his teeth over my small finger.

"Don't hurt me," I said.

"I'll never hurt you." He pulled me toward him and kissed me on the mouth.

We kissed for awhile, until our kisses grew more passionate and an ache grew inside me and I had the feeling that kissing would no longer satisfy the strange stirrings that rooted inside me. Esteban touched my breasts while I sat perfectly still. I did not know what to do; I could not identify these new feelings. I found Esteban's mouth and searched for his tongue.

When Esteban started unzipping my dress, I tried to pull away, but he whispered, "It's all right." And he slowed down and stroked my cheeks and kissed me long on the mouth. By the time he started fondling and kissing my breasts, I did not want him to stop.

One thing led to another; it is not necessary to elaborate but one day I found myself pregnant and even though Esteban tried to squirm out of it, we got married. I thought we'd be happy forever, like the fairy tales where the prince and princess live happily ever after. You see, before I found God, I believed in fairy tales and those saccharin love stories on movies and radio soap operas.

In less than six months, Esteban started hanging around with his friends in clubs, and before long he had girlfriends. It's a familiar story; a lot of other wives have had to put up with it. But while some wives could be passive about the matter, I wasn't. I would stay up until he came home and our early morning quarrels became fodder for gossip. I would rummage through his things, and took to weeping when I came across love notes in his briefcase; and I went crazy when I found lipstick on his dress shirts.

Tormented, I started spying on him. At first I would call his office several times a day, to insure he was working and not gadding about in some hotel room. Not satisfied with that, I'd go to his office at five and wait for him to leave. I drove my own car, and so did he; and I would trail behind him. Most of the time, he'd see me and head straight home. But once, he went to the coffee shop at Magellan Hotel. I parked and rushed into the coffee shop just in time to find a young girl sitting down beside him. If I had a gun I would have killed them, but thank God, I only had my ill temper and loud voice, and all I did was scream and carry on.

Esteban horrified at my behavior settled down for a little while at least, around the time I had the baby. I thought our problems were ended with Mariquita's birth. She was — no other word describes her — an angel. But God must have wanted to punish me, and Esteban too, because from the start, she had many medical problems. Then, when she was four, the doctors said she had leukemia. To Esteban's credit, he never got in my way of providing Mariquita the best medical treatment. We did our best but she became pale, thin, and her hair started falling out. Shortly after her seventh birthday, she died. The day before God took her, this little girl who was no more than skin-and-bones, she had kissed me and told me she understood she would die, that I should not be sad, that she was sorry that she would have to leave me behind. She said she hoped God would turn her into an angel so she could watch over me day and night.

It was too much for a mother to take. After her death and for years afterwards, I pretended she was alive. I kept her room exactly as it had been.

The servants were afraid of her room. They said the room was haunted. They said they sometimes heard a child playing. They refused to enter her room. I screamed at them, saying there was no ghost in there, and if there were one, I would welcome her, welcome her, welcome her. I alone cleaned her room. As if performing a sacred ritual, I would remove her toys from her bed, then I would pull off the ruffled bedcover and shake it out. Very carefully, I would cover the small bed with it, tucking it just so, under the pillows so it looked nice and fluffed-up. One by one I would lay her toys back on the bed, against the pillow: there was the monkey that she liked to drag around; the teddy bear with the bell inside; the pink elephant whose trunk she used to suck and which really looked quite disgusting but which I would hold as if I were holding on to life itself.

After making her bed, I would dust her dresser and arrange her baby powder, baby lotion, comb, and hairbrush. The bookcase came next and this took some time because I would read aloud her favorite books: the alphabet book, number book, Grimm's fairy tales, Bible stories, and many more. I would air out her closet. Sometimes I would polish her clean shoes.

Esteban called me mad. I did not care. I stopped caring for Esteban then. He could go with his drinking companions; he could wallow in the gutter with his women; he meant nothing to me. It was only Mariquita who meant everything to me and she was gone.

My aunt, my cousin, friends, talked to me. They said I had to pull myself together; I was still young; I couldn't throw my life away.

I followed their advice. I went to work at the American base. It was something to do, some reason to get up in the morning at least. There I found out I was still attractive, and I'll admit I had affairs. It made the time pass; it kept me from staring at the ceiling at night and thinking of my Mariquita in that cold, cold coffin.

For a while I was all right, but one rainy night, the sound of the rain on the roof was driving me crazy. Just this regular pitter-patter, pitter-patter, over and over again. I put some music on — *Rachmaninoff*, then I went to Mariquita's room. I could almost hear her playing and laughing. Her laughter was the most wonderful sound in the universe. The memory of it plunged my soul into darkness. In that murky darkness, the idea came to me then that I could end all this sorrow. I got a pen and paper and wrote Esteban, telling him my reasons for taking my life.

After, I went to the closet and spent some time deciding which dress to wear. I finally chose an old red dress, opting not to ruin my party dresses. After changing, I went to the bathroom; I locked the door; I selected a new razor blade. I was scared, but it was like falling down, you can't stop mid-way. I worried about keeping everything as tidy as possible. The only solution was the bathtub. I draped myself over the tub, my arms extended over the tub; but I was afraid I wouldn't be able to keep my arms over the tub, so I stepped into the tub and sat down. I held the razor blade in my right hand and found a vein in my left wrist.

And then I felt free, euphoric almost. The memory of Mariquita was in my mind, and I imagined myself floating up to her soon. I made the slicing motion as if it were all in slow motion. When I saw my red blood, I was glad I wore my old red dress. I blacked out and came to only when the maid screamed.

That was how I ended in Room 213 of Ubec General Hospital, under the care of Doctor Veloso. I was delirious for several days, but I became stronger. Then one morning, when I was almost fully recovered, I opened a drawer of the side table and found a bible. And this time, God yelled in my face. I picked up the bible and it fell open:

"Before I formed thee in the belly I knew thee; and before thou camest forth out of the womb I sanctified thee, and I ordained thee a prophet unto the nations."

I could no longer deny God's call; I had to stop running; I was His. Praise God!

Luisa and Nestor
(1930)

Luisa met Nestor Hernandez for the first time one day in May during the town's fiesta. Luisa's sister, Bianca, who had always taken Luisa under her wing, had asked her to come along. Bianca and her friends were older, but Luisa didn't care. Luisa considered it a privilege to spend time with Bianca. Bianca had a string of beaus and was always invited out. Many times Luisa would watch Bianca get ready for a dance; Luisa was the one who ran here and there for her freshly-ironed dress, or for gardenias for Bianca's hair. Bianca had flare. She could take an old dress and do things to it, add rick-rack or embroidery, and turn it into something that looked like a designer dress from Manila. Luisa loved Bianca's clothes, her perfumes, her makeup, everything about her. Bianca was also generous, not only with her things but with her time, because she used to help Luisa with her schoolwork and talk to her. Luisa wanted to be just like Bianca.

For the fiesta, Bianca had lent Luisa a long dress with multi-colored flowers along the scoop neckline, quite daring. It was a dress their mother would have disapproved of, but she never saw the neckline, thanks to Bianca's shawl. Their mother had grown up in an orphanage run by nuns and her strict ways were second nature to her. If the girls asked permission to put lipstick on, her answer was no; if they wanted to wear stockings, it was no. She did not allow them to "run around like party-girls." It was bad enough her five daughters were collectively called the "Delgado girls"; she didn't want to reinforce the aura of frivolity in their family. Fortunately their mother was always busy with her business and could not always keep track of the girls. Luisa and her sisters behaved in her presence but were mischievous when she wasn't around. Bianca got away with murder because early on she had made it clear that she would do as she pleased. She and their mother had numerous fights but their father defended Bianca, and their mother's resistance wore thin. Bianca was Luisa's salvation.

After shortening the hem of Luisa's dress, Bianca reddened Luisa's lips and cheeks with juice from native berries. She swept Luisa's hair up and held it in place with huge hairpins. Bianca stuck sampaguita flowers in her younger sister's hair. All the way to the town's plaza, Bianca's three friends complemented Luisa for appearing older than sixteen, and indeed Luisa felt very grown-up. They invited her to sit with them around the dancing area; but since Luisa had never danced before she sat behind them.

What she enjoyed watching the most was the flower dance. The flower dance was one way the town raised money. Eight local beauties, whose families contributed money for the privilege, were designated princesses for the night. They wore elaborate long gowns and had glittery crowns on their heads. With a lot of flair they were introduced one-by-one and then they sat on the stage. Throughout the night, the men could bid for dances with the princesses. Tipsy and generous, they would pay up to a hundred pesos per dance. The girls were so popular, they did not have ten minutes to rest. Luisa watched them, feeling both awe and jealousy. They were dazzling, so far above her; she knew her parents would never have the kind of money to buy her the title of princess. Even before this moment, she had figured out where they stood in the social totem pole of Mantalongon. Early on, she had decided that one day she would have the money and social standing that she did not now have.

Sometime during the flower dance, she was surprised when a young man approached them. Luisa had seen him around; he belonged to the Hernandez family that owned the biggest house in Mantalongon. He was Bianca's age, and Luisa expected him to dance with Bianca or her friends. Instead he came around to where she was and asked her to dance. Luisa sat transfixed, not knowing what to do. Bianca, who had seen what was happening, laughed and said, "You've got to dance sometime. Take care of her, Nestor. This is her first dance."

They were in the middle of the dance floor and he was turning her when she stepped on his feet. Wincing, he said, "You've never danced before?" She wanted to lie and say, of course I have, many, many times, but the words did not come. She blushed and turned her face to avoid his eyes. He danced with her only once, and she was sure it was because she had hurt him. Later when she went to get something to drink, she caught him smiling at her. She imagined he was making fun of her, and she felt her cheeks flush. The rest of the night, she would occasionally catch him watching her. She decided she hated him, but back home all she could think of was the feel of his arms around her, how he twirled

54

her around the dance hall, and how the string of lights overhead made everything look like something out of a fairy tale.

The next day Bianca's friends teased her about Nestor. Luisa dismissed the matter by saying, "Oh, I'm too young for that sort of thing." With the air of a sophisticate, Bianca declared that Nestor liked Luisa, and true enough the morning was not over when he appeared on horseback in their front yard. Bianca, who was out on the verandah, greeted him. She rushed into the house to tell Luisa that Nestor wanted to take her horseback riding. "Be back in two hours," she ordered.

"But what will I say, what will I do?" Luisa asked. Giggling and laughing, the girls shoved her out the door. Luisa wanted to run back in but it was too late. There he stood beside his horse, smiling at her.

"Be careful that she doesn't fall off the horse, Nestor," Bianca called.

Nestor helped Luisa up the horse, and he sat behind her. He wrapped his arms around her to make sure she would be safe. He was the first boy close to her and she found herself conscious of his warmth, of his smell, of his breath against her neck and hair.

He brought her all around town, and then they rode toward Pagsama Falls. There he left his horse with a caretaker and they started walking up the mountain. It was the first time they were alone together, but he acted as if he'd known her all his life, pointing out landmarks, holding her arm to make sure she would not fall into the water. In Luisa's eyes the place was enchanting. The splashing of the water was spectacular; a rainbow arced near the falls. The pools underneath the falls were clear and green.

Near the source of the spring, he said, "Luisa, let's run away and get married."

She laughed. "I'm only sixteen."

"I don't care. Let's elope right now."

"I can't do that," she replied, still laughing.

Then he took her face in his hands and kissed her gently. It was the first time she ever kissed a man, she felt faint. Something stirred inside her that she had never felt before. Even though she was afraid of what was happening to her, Luisa offered her lips to Nestor once again. Near the spring of Pagsama Falls, Luisa fell in love for the very first time.

Going to the Manila Hotel
(1939)

Luisa had heard about the extravangances of the Manila Hotel from her sister-in-law, Isabel. This same sister-in-law had made fun of the tiara she had worn at her wedding. "Oye, Luisa, you look like a queen!" Isabel had said. Luisa had not missed her mocking tone, and ever since had disliked Isabel. She tried not to show it because her husband's family intimidated her. Fermin and rest of the Sanchez family were all born with the proverbial silver spoon in their mouths, while Luisa grew up on carabao's milk and hand-me-down clothes.

Luisa had met Fermin when she was nineteen, a time when Nestor was two-timing her. Fermin had visited the mountaintop town of Mantalongon as the mayor's guest; and the mayor, knowing Fermin was a bachelor immediately brought him to Luisa's house. Fermin was overwhelmed by the beautiful women of the household. Luisa, the third of the Delgado girls had not expected Fermin to court her. He was much older and was a very serious businessman. She expected him to court her older sisters. But as it turned out, he started coming around, bringing gifts for her. Luisa found this flattering especially since Nestor was seeing Cora in Manila. Luisa knew his parents had something to do with Nestor's new attitude, that they thought she was not good enough for them. Cora came from a wealthy Chinese family in Manila. The whole thing burned Luisa up, and when Fermin asked her to marry him, she said yes, knowing this would break Nestor's heart.

Luisa and Fermin settled in the city, and her new duties as his wife kept her occupied. More precisely, she got busy shedding her provincial ways. She fired her dressmaker and acquired a couturier. But even the most expensive couturier of Ubec could not eradicate Luisa's love for flounces and brilliant colors, two more things that made Isabel smirk.

No matter, Luisa went ahead and spent Fermin's money to make herself look rich. She realized she could never look "Old Rich," but rich was rich. Luisa also liked to hobnob with the wealthy, which Isabel called "social climbing." But here again Luisa didn't give a centavo: she had her diamonds, her designer clothes, and she wanted to show them off to the very people who could tell the difference between the fake diamonds on her wedding tiara and the real ones.

Manila Hotel — Isabel said it was the grandest hotel in the entire Philippines, that it could almost compete with the fabulous hotels in Madrid, Paris, and London. Dignitaries visiting the Philippines always stayed at the Manila Hotel. It was perched right on the legendary Manila Bay where the sunsets were the best in the entire world. The more Isabel raved about it, the more Luisa hankered to go there.

Her opportunity came when Fermin mentioned he had to attend a board meeting and dinner of the Filipinas Sugar Cane Association at the Manila Hotel. Luisa told him she wanted to go. Fermin acted surprised, "Why, you've never been interested in these business matters before."

"It's the Manila Hotel, Fermin. I want to see it. Isabel says it's the most fabulous hotel."

"But-but it's just a business meeting, really quite boring, sugar production, that sort of thing. Then a reception, and that's it."

"I'll go shopping while you have your meeting, and I'll attend dinner," Luisa declared. She missed Fermin's resistance to her accompanying him as well as his nervousness in the coming days. She rushed to her couturier to have some dresses made, including a peacock-blue long gown; and she had matching shoes and bags made.

They sailed to Manila on board the Sanchez Lines, in the executive cabin since Fermin's family owned the shipping lines. In Manila, they occupied the penthouse suite of the Manila Hotel, which had a balcony overlooking the bay.

Luisa was surprised when Fermin went shopping with her in the morning. They went to Escolta and Fermin led her to the Star of Siam Jewelry store, where to her even greater surprise, Fermin bought her a five-carat diamond solitaire, with matching earrings, necklace, and God-bless-his-heart, a diamond tiara, smaller than her wedding tiara, but this one was made of platinum and real diamonds! Right then and there Luisa kissed Fermin, and for the rest of the day, she couldn't fathom why Fermin had showered her with such luxuries when it wasn't her birthday nor was it Christmas. Very briefly, the thought that his generosity appeared like the actions of a guilty man flashed through her mind, but then it was late afternoon and she had to get her hair and nails done at the Crystal Palace. Sitting in the shop, with three people pampering her, she imagined herself in her peacock-blue long gown and her diamonds, and she thought to herself that she at long last had made it to the top with the Zobels and Ayalas.

Dinner was held at the Orchid Room of the Manila Hotel, and all Fermin and Luisa had to do was walk down from their penthouse suite. They were stylishly late and by the time they arrived, everyone was present. A rumba number played in the background. Near the doorway, Luisa spotted a woman standing by a potted palm. When she caught sight of Fermin, she rushed over and kissed him on the cheek. Fermin pulled away, cleared his throat, and proceeded to introduce Chi-Chi Ibañez. Perhaps it was Fermin's nervousness, but a strange feeling crawled up Luisa's spine. She watched Chi-Chi fidgeting with the butterfly sleeves of her beaded wine-colored terno. Chi-Chi was tall and slender and several years younger than Luisa.

"I've been wanting to meet you," Chi-Chi said, addressing Luisa, all smiles.

Luisa felt Fermin withdraw, growing extremely quiet and reserved. He held her hand.

Luisa ignored Chi-Chi. "Your hand is clammy," she snapped at Fermin.

"It must be the humidity. You know Manila —" stammered Fermin.

"Humidity, my foot!"

"Luisa, please —" pleaded Fermin. The business of Chi-Chi was all out in the open; he knew that.

Fermin took his handkerchief from his pocket and mopped his brow that had sprouted enormous beads of sweat.

Chi-Chi persisted. "Fermin has told us about you, how truly Visayan you are —"

Luisa looked to see who "us" meant and found Chi-Chi's husband in a wheelchair beside her, a docile old man clearly paralyzed. And then Luisa lost it. Turning to Chi-Chi, she said, "I can't believe it. You slut."

Chi-Chi turned as white as the walls of the Orchid Room. A palpable silence settled around them.

"Here you have a husband, a sick man at that, and you have the nerve to run around with mine! You married him 'til sickness do you part, you take care of him and leave my husband alone!" Luisa didn't have a loud voice, but her voice boomed in the Orchid Room that night.

She should have stopped but instead she brought the matter one step further. Luisa grabbed a glass of French champagne from a waiter and dumped the contents on Chi-Chi's hair that wilted right before everyone's startled eyes. Chi-Chi grabbed Luisa's hair; and they pulled at each other's hair for several agonizing minutes until finally some men separated them.

On the way back to their room, Luisa shouted at Fermin, "Don't say a word!" She was regretting with all her might why she had married him in the first place. It was Nestor I really loved, she thought, not you.

Fermin's eyes were glazed; he kept quiet.

"So that's what those diamonds were about!" Luisa continued. By this time they were in their penthouse suite. Luisa stood in front of the mirror and stared at her reflection — black hair a frightening mess, her designer dress ripped up. She started crying. Fermin put one hand to her arm to console her. "Don't you dare touch me! Don't talk to me! Don't do a thing! Get out of my sight!"

Fermin heaved a deep sigh and retreated to his desk where he riffled through some papers. He kept this up for almost an hour while Luisa wept. Her crying must have worn her out because at some point she fell asleep. She awoke when the moon's rays hit her face. She glanced around and Fermin was gone. She thought surely he had left her, surely he'd gone to Chi-Chi for good.

What would she do? Luisa wondered. Her head hurt while she pondered her options. She couldn't return to her parents' house. Maybe she could kill herself; she could cut her wrist or jump off the balcony; but she felt life clinging to her and she knew she couldn't take her life. She could run away, perhaps to America or Spain. She wished Nestor were nearby so she could go to him, feel his comforting arms around her. But Nestor was grappling with his lousy marriage to Cora. That was when Luisa realized how far apart Nestor's and her paths had gone. At some point, even though they were married to other people, she still felt as if they belonged to each other, as if they could make up and get back together. But now she knew that they had created new commitments, entanglements, and bonds they couldn't sever no matter how strongly they loved each other.

During this time, Luisa felt as if her life were over, that she had nothing, absolutely nothing to live for. All the material things she had accumulated — the jewelry Fermin had given her, the gowns and dresses, the expensive furniture — they were meaningless. She was a woman abandoned by her husband for a hussy like Chi-Chi. She had been unable to keep Nestor, and now she could not keep Fermin. For all her good looks and charm (so people told her) she was nothing.

She kept at this for a long time until her eyes grew puffy and she grew tired crying. She got up and washed her face. She changed into her nightgown and went to the balcony. She shivered at the sight of the sea below, but the moon was large that night and she could not help staring at it and its twin reflection. Luisa was mesmerized. At some point, she forgot when because time had taken on a strange quality, the door rattled, and she grew frightened. "Fermin, is that you?" she called.

"Yes," he replied, softly, embarrassed.

"I wanted to make sure. You know, Manila, you can never be sure about big cities."

"Where are you?" he said.

"Out here."

"It's late. You should be asleep."

"I woke up and the moon was shining on my face. I was frightened. They say the moon's rays turn people into lunatics."

He came to the balcony and stood behind her. Several times he started to say something, but couldn't. Finally he blurted out, "My, that's a large moon." Luisa knew that he loved her still.

"I behaved badly — " she started.

"Don't worry about it. It's over."

"I know. But I feel so ashamed. What will your friends think? Your business, what will happen?"

"They'll think what they want to think. Nothing will change. They need our sugar."

"I was awful, just terrible. I can't believe I did that. *Madre mia*, just like a fishwife."

"Forget it, Luisa. I love you," he said.

"I know. I love you too." And surprisingly when she said that, Luisa realized a woman can love two men at the same time.

You know," she continued, "I didn't eat there, and I'm terribly hungry."

Fermin ordered chicken sandwiches and they ate them on the balcony, under the full moon. Later, they made love on the enormous bed in that Manila Hotel suite; and Fermin's affair with Chi-Chi Ibañez was ended once and for all.

In assessing the incident, Luisa Delgado Sanchez would say her life regained a sense of order once more; but if pressed, she would have to admit she experienced a loss that she couldn't pinpoint.

Wartime in Maibog
(1942)

When World War II broke out in 1941, Luisa and Fermin Sanchez had to evacuate Ubec city. They went to Fermin's ancestral home in the island of Leyte where it was presumably safer.

It had been a hectic retreat. Fermin had gotten word from the underground that Ubec would be the next target of the Japanese who had already gained a foothold in the Luzon area. The same night he heard the news, Fermin told Luisa to gather all their silver and jewelry and pack them in boxes. They buried these in their back yard. They locked up the larger valuable items — antiques and original paintings in one room — and entrusted the house to the caretaker. They packed some clothes and food and took off in a boat for Maibog, Leyte. Luisa had only visited Maibog twice during the ten years of their marriage. They were brief visits to attend the wedding of Fermin's sister and the funeral of his mother. Wartime was the only occasion when Luisa stayed in Maibog for a period of time.

What Luisa knew primarily about Fermin Sanchez before they got married was that he was extremely wealthy. Everyone in the region had heard of the Sanchez family and wealth. The Sanchez family had business holdings in three southern islands: Ubec, Negros, and Leyte. The family owned a shipping lines and a trucking business; it was a major shareholder of a beer company; it also owned numerous haciendas. Fermin had two brothers and a sister. One brother was retarded, so Fermin and his other brother ran the family businesses with his father. The three Sanchez men had divided southern Philippines so to speak, and Fermin's brother was in charge of business holdings in Negros; his father took care of Leyte, and Fermin had Ubec. Although Fermin's sister was a shareholder, she did not run businesses as the men did. She married a second cousin, and she and her family lived in Leyte near her parents.

The Sanchez ancestral home was called "the Yellow House" because it had always been painted yellow ever since the first Sanchez completed the European-style mansion on the God-forsaken place of Maibog, Leyte. Ramon Uno, as the first Sanchez was called to differentiate him from the numerous Ramon Sanchezes that followed after him, had obtained a Spanish land grant in Maibog. He had huge farm lands, but stranger though he was in this sleepy tropical place, early on he knew he would not make his fortune from hemp, sugar cane, and sweet potatoes. The agricultural products would allow him to live comfortably, but they would not make him rich. He had not left Sevilla just to be another sunburnt, well-off Spaniard; Ramon Uno's sight went higher than that; he wanted to be as rich as the kings of Europe. Ramon Uno looked at the sea and saw clear as day that shipping was his future. He made a big loan, built a pier, bought a few ships from Cavite and launched Sanchez Shipping Lines. The money started coming in. After he paid off his debt, he began constructing the Yellow House. Built three blocks from the sea, right along the town's main street, the house was patterned after a seventeenth-century palace, a breathtaking affair that stuck out like a sore thumb in the midst of the humble nipa huts of the town. A half-circle driveway led to the front of the house with its elaborate front doors that opened into an immense hall. An enormous crystal chandelier dangled overhead. Statues and planters stood in dark corners. Twin brass figures of Greek gods stood on pedestals at the foot of the stairs. Red carpet covered the mahogany stairs. Upstairs, more chandeliers hung in each room. The walls were covered with European wallpaper; the ceiling had intricate goldleaf design copied after the Castillo Montserrat in Spain. Sevres China, sterling service, crystal glassware, gold-gilt furniture, velvet draperies, lace linens, almost every single thing that you could think off came from Europe. The dining table was especially designed so it could open up and seat forty guests. There were eight enormous bedrooms upstairs and two guest bedrooms downstairs. In the west wing, a private chapel had hand-painted antique statues with eyelashes made from human hair. Beside the chapel stood a library brimming with leather-bound books. The ambiance of the place was so totally Western that one could easily forget that out there was a sleepy fishing village in the middle of nowhere in the Philippines.

It took three years to complete the Yellow House; and when it was finished Ramon Uno sailed to Sevilla to find a wife, a second cousin, a pale frightened young girl who ventured out of the Yellow House only to take care of her garden, which in time became renowned as the most fabulous garden in the entire Philippine Islands. By marrying his kin, Ramon Uno had started a precedent that continued for generations, and by the time it got to Fermin's generation, the Sanchezes had weakened their bloodline so much, they had retardation and blindness in the family.

Following the style of European royalty, Spaniards who came to the Islands intermarried among themselves to keep the wealth in the hands of few families. The Sanchezes followed this custom. The inbreeding problem was heightened when a male Sanchez fell in love with a local girl without knowing she was his half-sister after all, a bastard child of his father. The parents, terrified to reveal the truth, kept quiet. Brother and sister got married, and surprisingly their children were normal. However, a couple of these children married first cousins, and all of a sudden the abnormalities sprouted all over the place — dim-witted children, children born without pupils in their eyes. When these genetic defects were discussed, the Sanchez family would point out (as if it were compensation for the abnormality) that the blind ones sang beautifully; and indeed they were a force in the local church choir.

Growing up in Mantalongon, Luisa had heard stories of families intermarrying in this way. But she had never actually known families like that, and so the information filtered into her brain like fiction or folklore, along with the walking statue of the Child Jesus, and the enchanted beings that lived in ancient trees. She was quite astonished to see Fermin's retarded and blind relatives in Maibog.

She had known of Fermin's retarded brother and accepted this as the normal luck of the draw — families did produce Down Syndrome-children now and then — but she had not heard about all the others. She had not noticed them in fact when she had visited Maibog in the past, because the family kept them hidden from the public eye, tucked away in the proverbial family closet along with the other family skeletons. Fermin revealed the truth only when the Sanchez family got together for lunch shortly after they moved to Maibog and Luisa saw six handicapped Sanchezes grouped in a table with their attendants feeding them. Aside from Fermin's retarded brother, his sister had a blind daughter; and Fermin's aunt took care of a blind old man, a blind younger man, a retarded young man, and a retarded young girl. Understanding the embarrassment and difficulties they inflicted on their families, this aunt welcomed these unfortunate Sanchezes who came from all over the southern region. Also wealthy, she had a number of servants who helped care for these unfortunate relatives. They all lived in a huge white house (called the White House) next door to the Yellow House.

Stunned at the depressing sight, Luisa had excused herself and retired to the bedroom. Fermin followed her and asked what was wrong. She was crying. "This place is a menagerie. You tell me what's going on," she demanded. She knew Fermin had not told her everything about his family, and whenever she got annoyed with him, the memory of his one-time mistress Chi-Chi Ibañez always blossomed to fan her anger even more.

Reluctantly, Fermin revealed to her the history of intermarriage in the Sanchez family. She listened, horrified but also fascinated by the lengths the rich took to keep their wealth to themselves. She had believed naively that the rich became that way through hard work (as her mother had worked all her life, although her mother had never become wealthy).

"That is such a stupid thing to do, Fermin. Didn't they know what would happen if you marry your own blood?" asked Luisa who had grown up with dogs, cats, pigs, and other farm animals and therefore she understood the rudiments of genetics. She had seen a chicken with webbed feet; she had seen a puppy born with its heart outside its body; she had seen a cat with two tails, all from inbreeding.

Unable to explain what had become a way of life in his family for generations, Fermin lowered his gaze.

"And what if that happens to us? What if we have a child that ends up like them? It's just as well then that we haven't had one. White eyes, Fermin, they have white eyes. And don't tell me they sing beautifully!"

"You and I are not related, Luisa. I was aware of this problem, which was why I went out of my way to find a wife in another island. The chances of having similar genes increase when couples come from the same island; and when similar genes get together, that is when they become dominant. These peculiarities in my family will remain recessive in our children."

He said it: he married her for her genes, nothing more. Her distrust in Fermin flared up. To the world Fermin appeared the perfect husband. He was soft-spoken, kind, generous. He doted over Luisa; he provided her with every material thing she could ever dream of. But the world did not know him as she did. He was a hypocrite and a liar.

Despite her seeming gallantry in forgiving Fermin for his infidelity, she never really forgot nor forgave the matter of Chi-Chi Ibañez, no, not entirely. And now this business of the Sanchez abnormalities — or more precisely Fermin's lack of forthrightness about the matter, was another stroke in the debit side of Fermin's balance sheet in her heart.

She felt alienated from him and his relatives. In the past, the Sanchezes she had met (the women in particular) had treated Luisa with condescension. When Fermin's mother had been alive, she often commented that Luisa's ruffled dresses were too "provincial." She had even advised Luisa to stop going to her dressmaker and to go to the couturier Pitoy instead so she could have "better" clothes made. Fermin's sister had been another one who loved to tease Luisa for wearing huge pieces of jewelry. The other cousins and aunts (except the saint who took care of the handicapped) were no better; they always had some sugar-coated sarcastic remark targeted at Luisa, the gist of it being that she was a hick. Realizing the huge social gap between her family and theirs, Luisa used to feel overawed and kept quiet. They spoke fluent Spanish, French, and English; and it was true that they dressed impeccably, that they had the ability of flaunting their wealth without appearing gaudy, that they had style, that they had class; and they impressed Luisa. But now their wealth, their arrogance, their pretensions made her laugh inwardly. The famous Sanchez family was nothing better than a family of idiots. Now Luisa understood that their Castillian features, which they were so proud of, were the product of inbreeding, nothing more. High thin noses, white faces, dead-black hair — they never mentioned their buck teeth, wide hips and spinal curvature — in time they would breed themselves into monsters. She hated them all.

To top it all, this God-awful war had wrenched her away from her home, from people she knew and understood, from people who may not have been as filthy rich as the Sanchezes but who at least were normal. She felt dislocated and the yearning for Nestor Hernandez stirred in her soul once again. When Nestor returned in this manner, Luisa would remember him only in the best light. She would think of their happy times together; she would recall his adulation of her; she would taste the sweetness of their first love all over again. For some reason she never remembered the terrible hurt Nestor had done her. Nestor Hernandez had slipped into the realm of dreams and turned into a mythic being, perfect, unattainable. In Maibog during wartime, she nurtured this hankering for Nestor along with her desperation.

One afternoon, when everyone was away, she sat on the bench in the middle of the rose garden and wept quietly. Her heart was cracking, she was sure of it; and for a long while she wallowed in her misery until she heard singing. She paused to listen to the angelic voices and felt a lift in her soul. The music came from the White House and she realized that the blind ones were practicing. After that, she became intrigued with the singing ability of the blind ones and took to accompanying them to their choir practices. When she returned to the Yellow House from these practices, she would rave about their seraphic voices, voices so clear, so soothing, so absolutely rhapsodic. "Their voices are like liquid gold. And they are so docile, so helpless," she declared, clearly touched.

Fermin welcomed these moments of softness from Luisa, hoping she was getting over her anger at him and his family.

For a brief while, it seemed as if war would pass them by, but soon the Japanese reached this island, and the able-bodied men retreated to the mountains to join the *guerrillerros*. The rest stayed behind. When the Japanese army came through town, they appeared like ordinary provincial folks trying to survive; but the minute the Japanese turned their backs, they resumed helping the *guerrilleros*. The women helped run a makeshift hospital hidden in a nearby forest; and there they tended the wounded and maimed; there they prayed for those who died.

Nestor Hernandez, now a demigod in Luisa's mind, entered her life once again during wartime. A doctor in the guerrilla movement, he came to Maibog to deliver precious medicines. This happened early in the war. As luck would have it, Nestor and his party were involved in a skirmish with the Japanese. No one died on their side but his leg caught a bullet, and he arrived Maibog's hospital as a patient, not a doctor. For a week, Luisa took care of Nestor. There were other women around, of course, but the job fell on Luisa's hands since they had known each other during peacetime. And the truth of the matter was that Nestor was a terrible patient who would not stay put. He was prone to bleeding and was slow in healing. He was a complainer who gave everyone a bad time and only Luisa could pacify him. Acting crisp and cheerful as she imagined nurses to be, she cleaned and dressed his wound and took his temperature, telling him that she had to make sure he didn't come down with an infection. Amused, he would remind her that he was a doctor after all with a fine track record behind him. All the same, Luisa replied coolly, he was a patient in that place. It was all she could do to maintain a professional relationship with him; she did not want to fall apart in front of all the others. With people around them, both of them managed to focus on the concerns of other people: dwindling supplies, guerrilla tactics, Japanese atrocities, news about the Filipino and American armies; there was no time to dwell on themselves, no time to discuss the past, to figure out what had happened to the two of them.

On his last night in town, Nestor Hernandez made the mistake of stopping by to say goodbye to Luisa. Generally the Yellow House was filled with people, but that night, Luisa was alone. Fermin and his father were in the mountains; his brother and servants were at the aunt's house. If Nestor had known this, he would have been more prudent and would have stayed away, but there they finally were, just the two of them standing on the red carpet at the foot of the stairs. They kept a great distance between them; there was great fear in them.

"I'm leaving tomorrow at dawn," Nestor announced.

"I know," Luisa replied.

"Well, thanks for everything. I didn't know you're a good nurse."

"Are you sure the leg is fine?"

"It's healed nicely," he said, staring down at his left leg.

"Take care of yourself. Don't get shot at again."

"If I do, I'll come back here so you can take good care of me."

"Was I really a good nurse?" Luisa asked. She stood with her arms folded in front of her, her head tilted to one side, a stance she used to assume in her youth when she felt uncertain about herself.

He smiled, moved closer to her and pushed a lock of hair away from her cheek. "Yes, you were a great nurse."

"You were not a good patient," she said, pouting.

He stroked her hair. She smiled, remembering how it was in the past, and she must have turned her face towards him when he quickly pulled his hand away. "I have to go," he said, gruffly.

He walked toward the door.

"Nestor, don't get angry. I was just joking."

He stopped, turned around once again and met her. "I'm not angry Luisa. On the contrary, I am still very much in love with you. I have to go, Luisa, because I'm afraid of what I'll do if I don't go."

From inside the Yellow House, she pressed her nose against the windowpane and watched her demigod limping away, the distance between them growing wider. The thought crossed her mind that he would die and she would never again see him. She had seen quite a number of dead people — stiff, cold, unyielding, forever silent — and the idea of Nestor dead broke her composure. She could not stop herself; she opened the door and called him back. The situation was impossible for two people who had loved each other for over a dozen years. On the ancient double-poster bed in the guest room, they made love for the first and only time. The room had wide windows fronting the fabled Sanchez garden, and the breeze blew in the succulent scent of gardenias and ginger flowers. The kerosene lamp flickered on the table. Luisa felt for the first and only time the warmth of Nestor's skin and smelled his musky-man smell, and she tasted his mouth and body; and she felt him on top of her so they were one person; and she felt him inside her; and she felt a power over him that she had never experienced before he came inside her.

For a while, Luisa had romantic notions that he would return, but their daily struggle to survive consumed her energy. That single moment of lovemaking with Nestor turned into a kind of dream, and it flickered and faded beside the vivid and harsh reality confronting her. Years later that moment would merge with her memories of the war years, which she categorized as "madness"; and it was an incident rarely remembered.

As the war progressed the Japanese became more ruthless, and she and the others were always at edge, wondering if the Japanese would barge into their homes and rape their women and kill them all. Even though they lived in the province and had more food than city-folk, food became scarce. When Luisa missed her period, she brushed the matter aside; it was common for women to miss their period from stress and poor nutrition. But when she started getting nauseous in the mornings, she counted back and realized Nestor was the father of the child forming within her. Her initial reaction was shock, then fear. If Fermin and the world learned about the truth, they could destroy her. Fermin would leave her; Luisa would be alone, wartime at that, what would she do?

Luisa considered getting rid of the child. She could go to the local midwife, ask for herbs to end the pregnancy; she had heard of women who had borne seven, eight children, who refused to carry more and had done this sort of thing. It was not too unusual, not too frightening; she could do the same. But even while her mind wrestled with her problem, they were faced with day-to-day crisis — Japanese soldiers coming through their area, people getting hurt and needing care in the hospital, running out of food and digging roots to eat — and time passed, and before long the child moved inside her. It was a soft, fluttering motion, barely perceptible, but Luisa knew the baby was alive and she could not bring herself to kill it.

She kept her pregnancy a secret until the day a Japanese patrol stopped by Fermin's aunt's house. The three out-of-place mansions belonging to the Sanchezes had always attracted the Japanese passing through town. Usually, the soldiers stayed long enough to eat and rest. This time however the Japanese captain got it into his head that the aunt kept a short-wave radio. The soldiers searched the place, and finding nothing, they methodically tortured the people in the household to reveal the hiding place of the radio. The retarded ones did not even have the ability to answer with any kind of sense at all. Frustrated at not getting the reply they wanted, the Japanese beheaded everyone, each and every one of them, including the retarded one who smiled as the bayonet pierced his heart. By the time the *guerrilleros* arrived, the Japanese had moved on to the next town. Luisa and Fermin could do nothing more than arrange to have the bodies sent to the mortuary. It took them three hours to clean up the blood and put the place back into some kind of order. After having witnessed this horror, Luisa was feeling brave and reckless, and she decided to tell Fermin the truth. (What was the worst that could happen? she thought. If it was death, she had just stared at it face-to-face that day.) Walking back to the Yellow House in the dark, Luisa had reached over and touched Fermin's arm. "Fermin, I'm pregnant — " she paused, unable to blurt out the father's name.

Fermin stopped walked.

"Fermin, Fermin, are you all right?"

"Luisa, when I saw all those bodies tonight, I felt hopeless. War is remarkably stupid. I cannot understand why people haven't figured out that simple fact. It doesn't require a genius to understand the inanity of war. Generation after generation, we continue to do this, and we lose our sons; we lose civilians, many people. Not only that, we lose our homes, our dignity; we learn to hate. Tonight I had lost all hope. My aunt never hurt anyone in her entire life. She dedicated herself to taking care of my relatives. And those poor relatives of mine, what did they do to deserve that death? I felt desperate, but now I feel as if I have not lost it all, Luisa. Despite this madness, there is still something beautiful that managed to survive. Thank you, Luisa, for this child."

Luisa did not tell Fermin the truth. Until the day he died, Fermin believed Magdalena was his daughter.

Shortly after she told Fermin about her pregnancy, Luisa dreamt of a beautiful baby girl with the tail of a fish. In her dream, Luisa was concerned that the baby would end up blind like the unfortunate Sanchezes and so she checked the baby's eyes. She was relieved to find that the infant's eyes were normal. But the fishtail was another matter. Without feet, how could her baby walk? Since war had broken out, they did nothing but walk. There was little petrol around, and the few horses had been spirited to the mountain hideouts of the *guerrilleros*. In her dream, Luisa had pondered on this question for a long time until she finally figured that the baby would have to live in water.

She thought the dream meant her baby would have some kind of deformity. Fermin tried to calm her, but Luisa spent many mornings in church, praying that God not punish her by giving her an abnormal child. The midwife helped deliver Magdalena. With the authority of one who had delivered hundreds of babies, she declared that Magdalena was underweight but otherwise healthy. Fermin, who had nurtured his own private fears, heaved a sigh of relief; but Luisa peeled open the baby's eyelids and she counted the baby's fingers and toes, and she snapped her fingers next to the baby's ears to assure herself that the infant was indeed normal.

There had been nothing extraordinary about the birthing, although an incident shook the household soon after. Luisa woke up one dawn to Magdalena's gurglings, and she got out of bed and padded over to the crib. Still half-asleep, she bent over to pick up the infant and was startled to feel something cold and slimy. She opened her eyes wide and found a snake curled up next to the infant. Luisa screamed. Fermin got up from bed and saw the snake slither under a crack in the room. He grabbed his gun, planning to shoot the snake, but his father, who had entered the room to check on all the commotion, advised against it, saying the snake was Magdalena's twin, and the fate of the snake would be connected to Magdalena's fate.

From the start, Luisa had not been comfortable handling the baby. She tried breast-feeding but gave this up, saying she did not have

enough milk and her nipples hurt too much. They found a *ya*
care of Magdalena's need. Luisa found herself in a position w.
yaya would bring the baby to visit her several times a day, an
would coo at Magdalena and hold her for a short while, but quickly
turn her over to the *yaya* the minute Magdalena fussed or cried. It was
Fermin who checked on Magdalena's development, who fussed over
her, who talked and played with her. One of Fermin's cherished
memories was of the toddling Magdalena, sitting on the verandah
cane- chair, short legs swinging back and forth, as she waited for him.

After the war and when Magdalena was old enough, it was Fermin
who decided to send Magdalena to St. Catherine's College, an
exclusive girl's school ran by Belgian sisters. It was Fermin who would
go on shopping sprees at Escolta, buying Magdalena lace and
embroidered dresses, cowgirl outfits, walking dolls, peeing dolls, furry
stuffed toys, gold bracelets and necklaces, anything at all that he
thought would make Magdalena happy. And the child loved them all;
she chortled and giggled and laughed at every gift Fermin presented
her. During a rare moment of humility, Luisa wryly commented that
the major difference between Magdalena and herself was that
Magdalena grew up rich unlike Luisa who had to learn how to be rich.
But she did not begrudge the closeness between Fermin and
Magdalena. She accepted it as payback of sorts for the fact that Fermin
was not Magdalena's biological father. Many times, especially when
Magdalena was small, Luisa would study them fascinated at how two
people could be so intertwined they seemed to breathe together.

The sight of the two of them happy together was what gave Luisa
the courage to keep her secret locked inside of her.

Going to the River

The last time Luisa had seen Nestor was when Magdalena was four; and she, Fermin and Magdalena had gone to Manila on a holiday. They had driven to Antipolo to light candles to the Black Virgin; they had gone to Tagaytay to see Taal Volcano; they had spent a few days in Baguio with one of Luisa's sisters. Back in Manila, they visited San Agustin Church and strolled around nearby Fort San Pedro. They had watched Manila's fabulous sunset from the Luneta and had caught the sea breeze from the double-decker tram that cruised up and down the boulevard. At the tail-end of their trip, they went shopping in Escolta. At Capriccio's, Fermin bought a monsoon detector, a fancy gadget with metal dials that quivered at the slightest humidity change; Magdalena begged for and got roller skates; and Luisa found soft suede Italian shoes.

Fermin paid and picked up the bags with their purchases. Luisa held Magdalena's hand and the three headed for the front door. Right by the revolving glass door, with people milling all around them, they ran into Nestor and his wife, Cora. Luisa dropped Magdalena's hand, and her own hand flew up to cover her open mouth.

"Luisa," Nestor called, "do you remember me?" He was smiling widely, overjoyed.

"Nestor!" Luisa gasped, as she reached out and pulled Magdalena to her side.

"Your daughter? How lovely." Nestor bent down and smiled at Magdalena; the girl stared back at him. He winked at her playfully and she gave a shy giggle. Her hair was almost waist-long, and two heart-shaped barretts kept her hair away from her face. She wore a white pique dress with smocking. Magdalena looked like a calendar picture. "She favors you, Luisa," Nestor concluded, straightening up.

Luisa turned to Fermin. "Nestor Hernandez, Fermin. The doctor, do you remember, the war? The one with the hurt leg."

"Yes, of course, the guerrilla doctor. And how's the leg, did it heal completely?" Fermin asked.

Nestor flexed his knees slightly. "It's all right, but sometimes when it rains, it hurts."

"It's developed a bit of rheumatism perhaps," Fermin offered. "I have some rheumatism myself." Fermin rubbed his knees. "I've found that Sloan's Liniment works very well."

Cora's eyes glossed over Magdalena then lingered on Luisa — eyes as cold as those of a dead fish. Luisa felt a slight chill and she figured right then and there that Cora had heard of her, and she wondered how much Cora knew.

Luisa had been nervous herself, and the words had flown out of her head the millisecond her eyes fell on Nestor. When she recovered from the shock of seeing him, she resorted to stroking Magdalena's hair. She thought she ought to say something to Cora, something friendly or proper at the very least. She looked up and caught Cora chewing her lower lip. It was the first time Luisa had seen this woman who had stolen Nestor from her. She had white pancake makeup, which did nothing to improve her dry-looking face. She also had the expression of a sick cow; and those eyes of hers were dreadfully unfeeling. When Luisa smiled at her, Cora tightened her lips and her eyes threw little sparks. She looked so unhappy that even Luisa started to felt sorry for her. Luisa smiled wider, putting more generosity into her expression. After all, enough time had passed; and in balance, she had a good life with Fermin and Magdalena. Except for the Chi-Chi matter, Fermin wasn't a bad husband; and Magdalena was an angel, well-behaved and charming. Luisa was sure the three of them looked like the perfect family, unlike well, the two of them.

When Nestor suggested dinner together, Cora's fingers clawed into his upper arm. Fermin, oblivious to the drama in front of him, tried to work out a date with Nestor. Luisa ended the matter: "Fermin, the directors' dinner remember? I'm sorry Nestor, but our schedule is impossible."

Quickly, Nestor's expression became gloomy. He had wanted to see her again. But Luisa could not imagine their sitting through an entire dinner under such awkward circumstances. Cora would sulk. Fermin would be all right; he was always good with people. But what if Nestor stared too long at Luisa, or did something to show his affection for her? And worse, what if she did something to show she still cared? Just seeing him happy, with the sun shining on his head, made her want to run her fingers through his hair. She wanted to feel its thickness, its bushiness. She wanted to carress his face; after all this time and after everything, she still wanted to hold him.

Nestor's dark eyes dug into Luisa's. She lowered her gaze. If he probed hard enough he would know she still thought of him, still dreamt of him. In her dreams, he slips into her house. There is something furtive about him in her dream, as if he's a thief. He searches the house for something then leaves, and when she wakes up she feels as if she lost something important.

The day after running into Nestor and Cora, Luisa had chills. Fermin was worried but Luisa shrugged it off as influenza. She did not tell him that in her head Nestor became alive again. For months after, all she could think of was Nestor. She could not release him from her mind. Scenes of the times they shared haunted her day and night. She was exhausted. Once again, she imagined the life they would have shared if they had gotten married; she became angry at him for marrying Cora; she was consumed by old and new emotions, turbulent emotions. She thought she had gotten over him, but now their past hit her like a violent typhoon, and she felt as if she were mad. It took almost half a year before she could focus once again on her life. Half a year. It was too steep a price. From that time on, she wanted never to see Nestor again. She could not stand such torture all over again. Besides, she preferred that he remembered her as she was. Luisa wanted to preserve their past in a secret and beautiful place, untouched by reality. She swore then that she would never see Nestor ever again.

Now, in Mantalongon with Magdalena and her friends, Luisa felt Nestor's presence once again. She knew he was nearby, and so she declined going to the public dance to raise funds for the First Communicants. Despite the vivid descriptions of the banana stalks with bunches of yellow bananas, the string of multicolored lights crisscrossing the square, the band that had been practising the entire day, Luisa was firm about staying home. "I'm tired," she insisted.

When all of them left, even the servants, Luisa felt restless. Visiting Mantalongon always conjured up memories. She was not one who liked to dwell on the past. She believed that if you walk around carrying all that load, it is impossible to deal one-hundred percent with the present. After living all these years, Luisa figured it was the present that was real, not the past; neither was the future real, although she'd wager on the future over the past.

She roamed through the house where she had grown up, this house made of nipa and wood that used to embarrass her. The windows were the old-fashioned sliding type made of capiz shells. The floor was made of split bamboo; they had slept on mats on the floor. The house now passed for rustic and charming because Magdalena had fixed it up and because eight people weren't crammed in it. When Luisa had lived here, the house was crowded and decrepit. All the flowers that her mother had placed in vases to try to liven up the place could not hide their poverty.

She felt the presence of her past — her parents and her sisters. Her father had been a poet, a man whose head was up in the clouds all the time, a man who planted coconuts on his land so he could write his poems while waiting for the coconuts to mature and fall. Fortunately, her mother had some business sense and she wisely bought and sold salt, copras, hemp, vegetables, and flowers.

It took her years to comprehend the difficulty her parents endured to be able to provide their basic necessities: food, clothes, schooling. Five daughters — it must have been purgatory feeding and taking care of all of them.

Even when Luisa was young, she understood that they didn't have enough, which was why early on she decided that she would do better. And she did. She and her sisters succeeded. Luisa recalled with a pang how people used to say they married well because of their good looks, as if their parents prostituted them to wealthy men. They did no such thing. Naturally, men hung around their house; it was afterall a household with five good-looking girls. She and her sisters obviously had their pick, and, except for the unfortunate Sofia, they chose the right men.

Her favorite spot in this house had always been the verandah which ran the full length of the house. The roof extended over it so that even during the rainy season she could play there. "Market" was their favorite game; and she and her sisters used leaves for money, and they bartered and haggled the way her mother did in the open market. She could almost hear the noise of those children playing; she could almost see their happy faces. Luisa sat down on a wooden bench and looked out at the twinkling lights of the plaza. The faint pulsating beat of the band made her imagine the dancing, laughing, and drinking going on. In the morning, Mantalongon would have its share of drunks sleeping it off along its street corners. She recalled going to church one Sunday and wondering why men were sleeping against the church walls. Nestor, who had been with her, explained that those were last night's drunks. "Really?" Luisa said, surprised.

He had looked at her, thoroughly amused at her innocence, and he chucked her chin. Nestor used to laugh at the things she said or did as if she were the most delightful person on earth. Nestor, Nestor, Nestor, whom Luisa delighted, and who delighted her, until something went crazy and then they went out of our way to hurt each other. Sometimes she wondered if perhaps they were too happy and an evil spirit became jealous and set about destroying them.

She turned her attention away from the plaza and toward the rolling hill whose trees and shrubs were visible under the full moon. She could hear the faint rushing of the river at the bottom of the hill. She wondered if the river had changed much; and she yearned to put her hands and feet into the water. She fought this urge but finally surrendered. With just the moon to guide her, she meandered down the trail towards where the water splashed and tinkled over round, polished rocks. It was a cool night, and a slight breeze rustled the leaves of the trees and shrubs around her. Her footsteps must have woken the pigs in the shed because they grunted and rooted about for a while. She remembered their pet pig, Bruno, who would wander in and out of their house, a beloved housepet who generated quite a lot of tears when the time came for him to be slaughtered. She laughed at how she and her sisters had wept and worn black to mourn Bruno. What foolishness she and her sisters got into! As she approached the river, it was as if she could see Bianca and Sofia catching fish; she could see herself and Marta and Roberta helping the laundrywoman wash clothes in the river — phantom children, echoes of a past.

She sat on the rock by the side of the river and she studied the moon's reflection rippling in the water. How large the moon was, how yellow, how silvery on the shimmering water. This had been part of her world when she was young. She sighed. She was lost in the sound of the rippling water when a man called out to her. "Luisa," the man said, softly. "Luisa," with a faint tremble.

She became disoriented; for a while she thought it was a dream. Without opening her eyes, she knew who it was. "What are you doing here, Nestor?"

She glanced over her shoulder. Nestor was standing by the trail. The moon was above him and she could see that he was older, grayer, but it was still Nestor all the same. Certain things never change. She had accepted a long time ago that she would love Nestor until death, and that he would never forget her, never love another the way he loved her.

Seeing him there, sensing his yearning for her put a tremendous weight on her chest; she wanted to begrudge him for what he had done to them. They had been happy. What had possessed him to start seeing Cora? She had loved and trusted him, and that was what he had done to her?

"I wanted to see you. I heard you're in town." He walked toward her and sat on the rock beside her. "I had to see you."

He placed his hand on top of hers. His hand was warm. They were silent. For a long time, they gazed at the water that undulated under the moon and stars. To end the growing sadness around them, she said, "How did you know where to find me?" She pulled away her hand.

" I heard that your family's at the dance. I didn't think you'd go. I knew you'd come here instead. You always loved this place." He heaved a deep sigh.

"How is your father, Nestor?"

"You heard?"

Luisa nodded. "Sofia said he's not doing well."

He shook his head. "He struggles to stay alive. There seems to be something he wants to resolve, something, I don't know what exactly, but it disturbs hims greatly."

"I'm sorry. I'll light a candle for him."

"He wants to see you, Luisa."

"Me? Why would he want to see me?"

"I don't know why, but several times now he's asked for you. I tried to tell Sofia about it, but she wasn't in. I didn't really want to bother you, but he's dying. One, two days, no one knows for sure." He paused. "It's strange you know, you can hate someone all your life, only to find out you love him after all. Despite everything he is my father."

"Your father, not mine, Nestor. He is your obligation, not mine. I have no idea what your father would want to see me for."

"Neither do I, but maybe talking to you will help him go in peace."

"I'm sorry, it would be difficult for me."

He rubbed his temples and said, "You haven't forgotten."

"How can I forget Nestor? I was just a girl then, but I knew your father and mother disliked me. It will take a saint to forgive him, and I'm not one." She closed her eyes and shook her head. "I know this was many years ago, and I know I ought to forgive and forget. I have gone on with my life after all. But sometimes I still remember the look of contempt he gave me at the Fiesta de Mayo — do you recall? We were seeing each other then, and I was so happy to be with you, and I felt so glamorous and grown-up. He coldly stared at me and said he remembered seeing my dress on my older sister. Can you imagine saying that to a young girl? It hurt, Nestor, more than you can imagine. I knew, and the whole town knew what we were, but he didn't have to rub it in. I was so young; I couldn't understand the meanness. I don't understand it up to now. That was just a small matter. There was a bigger hurt he did me. I know he was responsible for what happened to us. He thought you were too good for me."

"He's sorry, Luisa."

Luisa laughed. "What does he have to be sorry about? He owes me nothing. The last time I saw him was in church. I greeted him, and we were fine. There was nothing wrong. Why would he want my forgiveness now?"

"I'm not sure, Luisa, but I think it has to do with us, with the past. He knew that we loved each other. He knows that I love you still. He's sorry for what happened to us — "

"If it's because he and your mother insisted on separating us, that they encouraged you to marry Cora, well, that was so long ago, Nestor. I have nothing to forgive. Besides you have paid the consequences, and are still paying for them; he should have asked for your forgiveness. "

"Forgive him, Luisa."

" I do not owe him anything; neither does he owe me anything. All these things are behind us now. Tell him I have nothing to forgive him for, that I have been happy all these years."

"Tell him yourself, Luisa, so he can die in peace."

She shook her head. "I can't. I have to go home. Our schedule's very busy. Magdalena needs me."

"You've become hard, Luisa. The girl I knew could forgive."

"The girl you knew no longer exists. Besides, I do not owe him nor anyone anything. I have done nothing but mind my own business. All these years, I have done my best to be a good wife to Fermin, to be a good mother to Magdalena, to do something good for the community. I have nothing to do with your father nor with you, Nestor. If he's in some torment, then he should pray directly to God. What good will it do him to see me? I cannot see him, Nestor. I could not handle it. The past is over. I don't want to bring it up again. Even seeing you now is very difficult."

"I'm sorry, Luisa. I didn't think you would be as upset as this. I'm sorry. Things are difficult at home with Papa the way he is. Everything is in turmoil. I wanted to see you and be happy even for a short while. I love you, Luisa. All these years, I've tried to forget you, but sometimes in the dead of night or in the middle of my work, I'll suddenly think of you. Cora and I have not been happy together. It has not been easy for me, Luisa."

"Then why — ? What happened? You yourself did not get along with him. You told me things, how he dominated you, how he favored Junior over you. You described how cruel he was to all of you. If he was so terrible, why did you do what he wanted you to do? Why didn't you stand up against him and tell him you loved me?"

"I don't know what happened, Luisa. It seemed like the right thing to do. Her parents, my parents all approved."

"And she was wealthy."

"It wan't that, Luisa."

"And I wasn't good enough for you."

"Don't say that."

"So what am I supposed to say? That you did what you did, and everything is forgiven and forgotten? Do you want me to say that the pain you gave me didn't count one bit? Besides it was true, wasn't it? Your family made sure I knew I was not worthy of you just because we were poor. Well, Cora had money, and you married for money and got what you deserved, Nestor."

"You will never know how much I have regretted what I did." He fidgeted, then changed the topic. "I heard about Fermin. It must have been hard on you."

"Yes, it's been hard, but he loved me, so I have something to hang on to even after he died."

"Were you happy with him, Luisa?"

"Yes," she said, meaning it.

He sighed again. "I should be glad you've had a good life. I have not been so lucky. You should not have married Fermin. I would have married you. I was just young and didn't know what I was doing."

"Nestor, what was I suppose to do? Sit around, while you ran around with Cora. That's not my type, Nestor. You should have known me well enough to know that I would get on with my life. At any rate, Cora wanted you more than I did. She really went out of her way to get you. She was always inviting you to this and that, and she pressured you to break up with me. It was clear that you didn't know what to do with both of us, and so I made it easy for you."

"That's all in the past. The important thing is that I love you still." He reached out to touch her face, but she pulled away.

"Don't start, Nestor. Don't. We made our choices decades ago. It's no use going over and over the matter. There is nothing we can do about it now. We'll go crazy."

"You will never know how much I think of you and hate myself for letting you go. Life has not been easy. I've survived on memories of us. Those memories are like air to me, Luisa. Tell me, do you love me too? Do you love me still?"

She wanted to say: What's the point? What's the point? I am fifty-five; you are fifty-eight; we have wasted a lifetime; you are stuck to a woman you abandoned me for, so what's the point? What do you want from me, Nestor? I gave you my heart, my soul — so what else do you want? What's the point?

Instead she got up and moved away from him. "I have to go. Nestor, please do not see me again. Our history is past."

"Luisa, wait, you say our history is past, but our story is not ended. I accept that you and I can never have the kind of life we talked about. You and I can never have the children we talked about. We can never have the dreams we talked about, a long time ago. And the irony of it all is that I realize I played a large part in destroying those dreams. That is what hurts me most."

"You were the one who two-timed me, Nestor. I waited for you."

"Luisa, I don't know what happened to us. We loved each other, and then the whole thing fell apart. My life has been filled with complications, convolutions, twists and turns; it has been a dark maze and often times I've lost my way in it. How I wish that my life were a straight path. Point A to Point B. But it is not that cut-and-dry; and this other thing I'm faced with, that I'm dealing with, is much more demanding, much more painful so I know it is not quite so simple, our story. Time and again, when I analyze our story, it 's like a mirage, and sometimes I start to get a picture but then it vanishes and I'm back to square one trying to figure out what in hell happened, why you ended up married to Fermin, and I to Cora. For a long time I blamed you for marrying Fermin, for abandoning me."

"I did not abandon you, Nestor. You abandoned me. You abandoned me not only once but twice. Two times. So don't rewrite history now."

"You have to understand that I was a student in Manila with few friends. I was a country bumpkin in Manila, a small fish in a big ocean. I had been somebody in Mantalongon, and suddenly I was nobody in Manila."

"Well now you are somebody, Nestor. A minister of something or other, I understand. You should be happy."

"Don't be so cruel, Luisa. I am trying to explain to you, as well as to myself what happened. It was not easy in Manila. Cora's family was a friend of my family, and they took care of me, took me places, invited me to parties, introduced me to the important families in Manila. The next thing I knew, well, there was Cora, you see; we had become a kind of an item in Manila. And the very next thing I knew you announced you were marrying Fermin. That one picture of the mirage I will never forget, of you telling me you were getting married. You looked so triumphant. You were cruel to me, Luisa."

"And were you fair with me, Nestor? I loved Fermin. He was good to me, unlike you Nestor, who humiliated me. How do you think I felt? And wartime, you entered my life once again, and once again discarded me as if I were a piece of rag. I waited for you; again I waited for you. You have no idea how I waited for you, day in and day out, until finally I realized I would have to go on with my life without you."

"After Mantalongon, I was sent to Mindanao. There was no way I could see you. When war ended, I heard you had a child. You have no idea how much I wanted to see you, but I figured you were settled with Fermin and your baby. I decided to leave you alone. It seemed the noble thing to do, to leave you in peace."

"Then why aren't you leaving me alone, Nestor. If you were a real man, if you were truly noble, you'd leave me alone."

"I came to ask you to see my father,"

"I can not see your father. You're stirring things up again. I've been fine, Nestor, fine without you. I have to go."

"Luisa," he said, restraining her, subduing her anger, "all these years, I have tried to separate the past from the present but never could. I could never look at the world nor could I relate to others without you present. All the time. All the time. You have been some kind of filter through which I've viewed and experienced the world and life. I love you, Luisa."

He moved towards her, took her into his arms, and without thinking, like instinct, she offered her lips to him. He kissed her; it was the same kiss of long ago, the same kiss by the source of the spring when he had asked her to elope with him and she had laughed and said, I'm too young. It was impossible to keep time in order — time rippled like the waves in the river, and for a while they were young again.

"I love only you," he repeated, and she could feel his heart beating against her, and she wished that life was like a Hollywood movie where the two of them could walk off into the sunset and there was no getting up the next morning because the next day and the day after, you would have to deal with your responsibilities and commitments, and really, they had missed their solitary chance a long time ago and never again would they have the same opportunity again, never.

When he started to kiss her again, she pulled away. "You're bringing all these things up once again, and you have no idea how much it hurts me. This is madness. I have my life in Ubec, Magdalena, my house, my friends. You have your life. There's Cora who needs you. This is crazy. I have to go." She started to walk away.

He followed, but she said, "No, Nestor. Let me go. It's over."

He stopped, and she walked away from him, away from her past and all its memories.

Doing One's Best

April Lim-Veloso Hernandez was the daughter of a Chinese immigrant from Canton, China, who was known in the Philippines as Ah Sin Lim but who had been born as Han Shan-chow. Han had trained as a grade-school teacher but quickly discovered he disliked children. He wanted to become rich, and it quickly became apparent that teaching was not the right profession for him. One of his uncles who lived in America used to write about the wonderful life at the Golden Mountain. This uncle would send pictures of himself in dapper suits beside gorgeous women, and once he sent a photo of himself standing in front of a shining Ford Model T. This uncle's colorful and glamorous accounts convinced Han that he should join the "Celestials" in America. Life in America sounded more interesting than teaching a bunch of unruly children. Besides there was money to be made because the railroad companies went out of their way to hire Chinese who were reputed to be hard workers.

Han set about saving money for his passage but just when he was ready to buy his ticket, his family received a letter from America informing them that the uncle died. The uncle, who worked for the Northern Pacific, had been placed in a wicker basket, lowered over the edge of a cliff so he could chip roadbeds out of solid rock. Unfortunately, the uncle fell out of the wicker basket and plunged down the steep cliff. The Northern Pacific bosses didn't bother retrieving his body, but they did find another Chinese worker to go down the cliff to continue the work.

Han saw the blatant injustice in what had happened and he wisely figured that the uncle had been giving them gilded reports of "life in America." Han decided he didn't have to go all the way to California to find his Golden Mountain. He chose the Philippines instead because many Cantonese migrated to the Philippines and made money there. After making the necessary contacts, Han was able to buy the identity papers of a Chinese man, Ah Sin Lim, who had just died in Manila. Renamed Ah Sin Lim, Han sailed from Canton and arrived in the Chinese district of Binondo one sweltering April day. Unlike many other Chinese, he had the luxury of entering the Philippines legally.

The new Ah Sin Lim quickly discovered that the Chinese were at the bottom of Philippine social ladder. He was dirt-poor, which kicked him farther down society's ladder, but he was young and hard working. He thought of a business, one that had been going on in China for centuries. He started a noodle-soup business, small-time to start with. He made his own broad noodles, and he searched for a long time for the perfect broth to go with his noodles. Chicken soup would do the trick, but he discovered that the American White Leghorns, which were the craze in the Philippines, huge though they were, tasted no better than boiled rubber. He used the smaller but fatter native chickens instead. He seasoned the broth with vetsin, put in his broad noodles at the last minute, and he had his perfect noodle soup.

Ah Sin Lim carried his containers suspended from the ends of a length of bamboo slung across his shoulders. On one end, he carried the broth, kept hot by live coals underneath; the other container held the noodles and boiled chicken, the bowls, and Chinese soupspoons. Looking like a coolie in his black pants and his long queue swinging down his back, Ah Sin Lim walked up and down Ongpin Street, along Gandara, Alonso, and F. Torres. By late afternoon when his feet and shoulders had had enough, he planted himself near Binondo Bridge. Hungry passersby would stop and order a bowl of noodle soup, called *gupit* meaning "cut." Ah Sin Lim's prices varied. One could place a five-centavo order or more, depending on one's appetite. Ah Sin Lim would hold his broad noodles over the bowl and using scissors that jangled from his belt would cut five-centavos worth of noodles that fell and nestled deliciously into his dragon-decorated blue-and-white bowl. He would also cut the chicken meat into the blue-and-white bowl, then pour steaming hot soup over the all thing. He would give his favorite customers extra noodles and chicken fat. No one ever questioned how clean those bowls and soupspoons were, even though Ah Sin Lim didn't always wash them properly; but the soup clung to their bellies and his customers multiplied.

From early morning until late at night, he worked, and after three years, he opened his first restaurant, called "Lim's Restaurant." It was an unpretentious place near the Luneta, but his soup was good and plentiful and the numerous promenadors out to catch the evening sea breeze along Manila Bay soon frequented his restaurant. His business took off and before long, he had several restaurants in Manila. By the time he was twenty-eight, he had acquired the title of Noodle King of

Manila, and was considered a "catch" in Manila's Chinese community. Several Chinese businessmen approached him to try and arrange a marriage between him and their daughters. Ah Sin Lim considered their propositions carefully. There was something to be said about making the right business connections in the Philippines, indeed there was a lot to be said about marrying into the right family. In addition, a Chinese wife who had grown up or had actually been born in the Philippines could prove helpful. She could help run his businesses; she could mingle with the Filipino customers; she could teach him how to conduct himself when he met the Filipino upper-crust because Ah Sin Lim had not yet gotten rid of the Chinese habits of spitting and slurping while eating, even picking his teeth in public. It was true that the wealthier he became, the more opportunities he had to meet wealthy Filipinos. They would eat at his restaurants and talk to him. A wife who could double his efforts could be a real asset.

In the end however, he turned them down. His mind was on a round-faced young girl with bound feet whom he had loved in Canton. Many, many nights, after he had massaged his aching shoulders (his left shoulder was shorter than his right, from carrying the bamboo pole) and finally lay his weary head down on his pillow, his mind would sail back to Canton, and he would fix on Ling-ling, recalling her mincing gait, remembering her exquisitely embroidered silk shoes, wondering what her little feet actually looked like, the mysterious Golden Lotus feet. On wanton nights, he would think of fondling, nibbling, licking and sucking her feet. Sometimes he would imagine dipping her feet into tea before drinking it; and he would think of eating almonds from between her crushed toes. When he was feeling very wicked, he would imagine making love to her and feeling her jade gate tightly grip his jade spear as women with small feet could reportedly do. He would raise her tiny feet to his shoulders and insert her Gold Lotus into his mouth and suck noisily until the moment of "Clouds and Rain."

He returned to Canton for the girl with bound feet whose memory sustained him during numerous lonely nights of his five-year odyssey. To his surprise the girl was no longer the slender undulating goddess of his dreams but a plump hobbling woman of twenty-five, who complained in her piercing peasant voice about her feet hurting. She described to him the torture she had been subjected to make her feet small. She had been only four when her father took her to the foot-binder. Her feet had been soaked in a broth of boiled monkey bones.

Her bones softened, her feet had been bound tightly in cotton bandages so only her big toes were left free. Her feet were rebound daily, tighter and tighter over the next two years, so her other toes were broken and forced flat against her soles, the arches broken, the heels drawn forward. It was torture, sheer agony, pure pain, and Ling-ling made sure everyone knew just how excruciating the entire business had been.

Ah Sin Lim should have understood that the target of his desire, the little pink dumpling feet of Ling-ling, were mere mutilations, but Ah Sin Lim could not get rid of the mystery behind her feet. Little dumpling feet had been imprinted in his mind as erotic objects and the mere thought of those miniscule feet raised his blood pressure and created havoc within him. He was ashamed to admit that some nights, he had gone to a particular house in Binondo with Chinese prostitutes, and there he had participated in their wicked game which involved handling the women's shoes while the women hobbled about barefoot.

He wanted Ling-ling still. Despite Ling-ling's hefty size; despite her shrill voice; despite the obvious signs of her dour disposition; despite the fact that she was now an old maid, he hankered for her. Ling-ling had been the object of his desire for too long. She could have been a toothless old hag but in Ah Sin Lim's mind she would still glow and shimmer from all the nights of imagining, all those painful nights of yearning to kiss her tiny Golden Lotus feet. Ah Sin Lim discovered something about himself then, and that was that he was terribly bullheaded. It was the same thing when he had made up his mind to get rich; he had almost literally broken his back, but he had gotten what he wanted. He had made up his mind that he would have Ling-ling, and he would possess her too, never mind the serious discrepancies between his fantasies and reality.

The family of Ah Sin Lim's passion, in particular the ambitious father, who had not thought much of the poor teacher Han, agreed to surrender Ling-ling. In the first place, Ling-ling had proven herself unmarriageable. (She was almost betrothed to an older man who mysteriously died the day the matchmaker was making negotiations, and ever since then, no one wanted to have anything to do with "Bad Luck Ling-ling.") In the second place, Ah Sin Lim offered the family a substantial sum of money, which they used to buy another farm — the family had had a solitary small farm. Ling-ling's family had never been wealthy in the first place; her bound feet had been her father's caprice, an investment in hopes that his daughter would marry a wealthy man, a way of social climbing.

Ling-ling's feet measured three tiny inches, which may have been the reason she hardly set foot out of their home in Binondo — this plus the fact that she rapidly gained more weight from her constant indulgence in sweet meats and dried candied fruits. She did not like the Philippines, not even Binondo which smelled of fish sauce and pork fat and which looked like a piece of China itself. She stayed in their house that was a replica of a Cantonese magistrate's house. It had an inner courtyard with a fishpond filled with koi. The rooms opened out to the courtyard. Teakwood furniture, porcelains, jade carvings, embroidered linens came from China; and what she could not get from China, she bought at a high price in Binondo, or had made by an old Chinese artisan who did not Filipinize nor Americanize his handiwork.

In this house she bore her solitary daughter, whom she turned over to an amah upon birth. Her daughter hardly knew her. Ling-ling never learned Tagalog, nor did she speak English. The daughter, whom Ah Sin Lim sent to the finest exclusive schools in Manila learned Cantonese, Tagalog, and English. Ah Sin Lim had also picked up Tagalog and English during his bamboo-pole days. When people visited their house, conversation was trilingual, with people slipping in and out of the three languages as they saw fit. Ling-ling was left out of these conversations. Her husband and daughter had to translate everything into Cantonese for her, a task they found arduous. Eventually her husband and daughter kept such gatherings and conversations at a minimum. Bit by bit, Ling-ling became almost like a fixture; she could have been one of her expensive teakwood furniture. Her husband and daughter would visit her as if visiting a shrine. They would talk to her, then take off and join the outside world that was becoming more and more their world, a world that had never been and would never be Ling-ling's.

Alone, she would remember the blue hills of Canton. From the time she left Canton in 1880 until she was killed in 1942 by an enthusiastic American soldier who mistook her for Japanese, Ling-ling never forgot China. Some nights she would dream of the Bei and Deng rivers and wake up with an unquenchable yearning to swim in their waters. To keep her pulse on Chinese developments, she followed Chinese news avidly, keeping track of the demise of the Manchu Dynasty and the subsequent revolutionary governments of Sun Yat-sen, Chiang-Kai-shek, and Mao Tse-tung. She never developed an interest in the Philippines' own broiling politics: the 1896 revolution against Spain, the 1899 Philippine American War, the American Occupation, and the fateful 1941 Japanese Occupation which brought about her doom.

Visiting China was out of the question of course. As Chinese citizens, their papers did not give them the liberty to come and go as they pleased in the Philippines. Besides, her husband was too preoccupied with his business. Unlike Ling-ling, he had made his life in the Philippines and wouldn't consider leaving even for a few weeks. Ling-ling with her tiny feet was barely mobile, and so the best thing she could do was to hire a local artist to do a mural of Canton on her bedroom walls. Lying on her three-sided bed, she would spend hours gazing at the painting while eating her sweet meats and dried fruits.

She became fatter still until she couldn't even hobble about but had to be lifted everywhere. When Ah Sin Lim started seeing another woman, Ling-ling attempted to save herself. She plucked her hairline to rid herself of her widow's peak and recapture the moon-face she once had. She ordered new silk gowns, billowy tents that hid her shapeless body. She also organized a mahjong group, but it was the same story. Most of her friends were trilingual and Ling-ling did not understand half of what was said during their mahjong sessions. Sitting outside in the courtyard, shuffling the ivory mahjong pieces around, they would wile away the night gambling and gossiping about their children, their husbands, and their husbands' affairs. Ling-ling struggled to keep up with the conversation — it was a strange sensation for her to hear people chattering away in Cantonese only to have them suddenly utter strange words, then Cantonese would flash back again, but Ling-ling had already lost the thread of the story. She was never certain which child went to what school, which child was dating whom, who was getting married to whom. Stories merged into a strange quilt stitched together in a haphazard manner, without planning nor design. More and more the mahjong sessions left her angry and frustrated. She finally gave up mahjong the night she suspected two of her friends of signaling each other in English to make her lose fifty-thousand pesos, a huge amount at that time.

Isolated, she started smoking opium, an addiction she maintained until 1942 when the nineteen-year-old Marine from Georgia, burst into her room, took one look at her on her kang bed, shouted, "There's a Jap here," and shot her. (The irony of the manner of her death was that even before World War II erupted in the Philippines, she had supported Chinese resistance against the Japanese; but it had not been unusual for American boys to confuse one Asian with another, to confuse friend with foe.) By that time, she had seen her husband start another family with his Filipina accountant, and she had seen her own daughter abandon Binondo and her, ashamed of her Chinese heritage.

The daughter had an American name that Ling-ling could not even pronounce properly — April. Ah Sin Lim had insisted on the name. April had been the month of his arrival in the Philippines; it was an auspicious name. He had had a fight with Ling-ling over the matter. In fact, by the time April was born, Ah Sin Lim had grown quite tired of his wife. The memory of her was far, far better than the reality. Ling-ling with her bound feet and incurably Chinese ways, was becoming something of an embarrassment to him. She was holding him back from his objective of "assimilation." Ling-ling would never be part of Filipino society. He provided for her in the house in Binondo, but he took on a Filipina concubine whom he introduced to people as his wife. He had another house built in Malate, far away from the Chinese district, and this household was run in a Filipino manner. His daughter April, whom he encouraged to act Filipino, split her time between this house and her mother's house in Binondo.

Ah Sin Lim had quickly figured out that even with money, a Chinese was always thought of as a Chinese in the Philippines. He was always discriminated against, sometimes in subtle ways, and sometimes not so subtle. Philippine laws discriminated against the Chinese, and immigration laws in particular made it difficult for Chinese to live in the Philippines. The Chinese had to resort to using dead immigrants' documents, as Ah Sin Lim had done when he bought the identity papers of the man whose name he assumed for the rest of his life. It was a peculiar situation and confusing. One was never sure if the Lee Chew or Wan Lee that people referred to was really that person or someone fresh-off-the-boat.

The Chinese could not own businesses in their names and could only hold forty percent of corporations or partnerships with the majority belonging to a Filipino. Consequently the Chinese entered into fake marriages with Filipino women so they could place their businesses and properties in their wives' names. There were many tricks the Chinese could do in the world of business. But the matter of Philippine society was another thing; and they found themselves being called insulting names. It didn't matter if they had amassed a fortune, children would still point fingers at them and utter the nonsensical ditty: "*Instik beho, tulo laway* — Chinese old man, saliva streaking down." Even though Ah Sin Lim's meteoric rise transformed him from the black-pajamaed street vendor to the chauffeur-driven hotshot sporting American suits, he would still find himself in the demeaning position of being dismissed as "*Instik quakang* — bowlegged Chinese."

The Chinese who had lived for some time in the Philippines learned to camouflage their heritage. Figuring their names were a dead give-away, they got rid of them. They gave their children American names such as George, Joseph, Dick, Jane, Mary, William (which was what inspired Ah Sin Lim to give his daughter an American name). Quite a lot of Chinese were named Robert Lee. There was another trick that earlier Chinese immigrants learned, and that was to get well-known Filipinos to be sponsors of their children at baptisms. The baptized child assumed the family name of the sponsor. For instance, Ah Sin Lim asked Congressman Antonio Veloso to be his daughter's sponsor, and April became April Lim-Veloso.

As part of Ah Sin Lim's assimilation program, April attended the exclusive St. Catherine's College in Manila where she hobnobbed with the Ayalas, Madrigals, and other Old Rich of Manila. In that environment, she decided to drop the Lim in her name and call herself April Veloso. Even though she rarely saw her sponsor, Senator Antonio Veloso, she referred to him as her "uncle." She was introduced to Jose Hernandez as April Veloso, at a rigodon ball at the Manila Hotel. Jose did not have to see April's mother in Binondo; he understood what the score was right away. But at that point of his life, he was into making money and April's money and connections helped blur racial differences.

With one meeting, Ah Sin Lim assessed Jose Hernandez to be cunning, and ruthless if necessary, traits that Ah Sin Lim recognized and respected. But far more important, Jose Hernandez was a Filipino, a mestizo at that. Ah Sin Lim's grandchildren would be Filipinos with the desired Spanish mix. His bloodline would be assimilated into the Filipino mainstream. No more of this *Instik beho* and *Instik quakang*.

There had been no pretenses about it, the marriage between Jose and April had been an opportunistic arrangement between the two parties. There had been occasional sexual encounters, which accounted for Jose Junior's and Nestor's existence, but overall it was a passionless alliance that focused on acquiring money and properties. Their conversations could have been between a businessman and his accountant: we spent this much last month and the food bill has gone up considerably, we'll have to trim someplace else, and so on. Like her father who had measured his noodles by the centimeter, April ran a tight ship where every centavo was counted. Even toothpicks were inspected to make sure the servants were not wasting them. It was a household where every single part of a chicken was eaten: head, eyes, feet, blood, intestines, everything; and the feathers were used to stuff pillows.

That was how April saw marriage, as primarily a business arrangement, and short of arranging her sons' marriages Chinese-style, she angled and maneuvered for what she considered good marriages for her sons. Thanks in large part to April's vigilance, Jose Junior and Nestor married women from wealthy Manila Chinese families; women who were mirror images of April. Both marriages turned out to be first-class disasters, a fact April simply could not fathom. If she and Jose could tolerate such an arrangement, why couldn't others? As far as she could see, she and her husband had built a financial empire, so why couldn't his sons and their wives do the same? When her sons complained that they were unhappy because they didn't love their wives, she said, "What is happiness? What is love? You can't eat happiness or love, you can't buy anything with happiness or love, you can't pay bills with happiness or love. Love and happiness are nothing."

But even though April knew little about love, she understood hate. She had grown up on hate. She hated being different from her classmates at St. Catherine's; she hated how people looked down on her for being Chinese; she hated how Chinese her mother was with her shrill Cantonese voice and her out-of-place flowing robes; she hated the Chinese house in Binondo; she hated being April Lim.

Jose Hernandez entered her life, and even if he were not exactly the knight in shining armor, he saved her from being April Lim all her life. When she met Jose, he was a machine whose sole purpose was to acquire more wealth and power. She too went along with Jose's obsession to become wealthier. It suited April fine; talk of money and material things was the language in her father's home.

She would, however, feel occasional pangs of jealousy when she saw happy women. She would stare at their glowing faces, their wide smiles, that soft expression which made her wonder if she had missed out on something important. She had never loved anyone with a passion. Love was never talked about nor experienced at both her parents' households. Love, as far as April was concerned, was akin to the enchanted beings that servants talked about — the whole thing just a lot of malarkey.

She did not know how to love her two sons, although she would never have admitted this of course. When they were growing up she insured that they were properly fed and clothed. The two boys had an *amah* until they were eight. But in the same way her mother Ling-ling had ignored her, April never played with the boys; she never read to them, she never talked to them, she never related to them. The boys were there, part of her duties as the wife of Jose Hernandez. She gave them huge allowances, bought them everything they wanted. She gave them obligatory scoldings, parroting other parents who nagged their children about their schoolwork or their manners. She had done her best; she could honestly say that. Even if she had pushed them into unhappy marriages, even though it was rumored that Junior committed suicide, even though she felt a gaping hole in her soul as she stared at Junior's mangled body, she could look anyone straight in the eye and say she had only done what any good mother would do. April Lim-Veloso Hernandez had done her very best.

Typhoon
(1912)

It was still dark when the sound of shattering glass cut through his deep sleep. Nestor held his breath at the sharp, splintering crash, and he turned his head toward the bedroom door and listened through the rain and wind for more noise. There were footsteps then the muffled voices of people. He wondered about the commotion and speculated these had something to do with last night's events.

Last night, the storm had not raged as violently as it now did. The wind had not howled as loudly through the pines and coconut trees. It had been different last night. Things had been all right yesterday, unlike this cold, dark, early morning. He could sense the change, smell the moisture in the air, feel the prickling tension as people padded back and forth and the house strained against the wind and lashing rain that fell in hard rapping sounds on the rooftiles.

He and and his brother had misbehaved; there was no doubt about that. Their father Jose had spanked them; their mother April had screamed at them; and worse, *Yaya* Taying cried and refused to talk to them, would not hold them in her arms, would not kiss them.

He felt like crying but did not want people angry again. Crying was something Junior often did; but it was not his way; and so he tugged at the end of his blanket and began to suck on it. He waited, hoping his *yaya* would open the bedroom door and sail in to pick him up from his crib, rescue him from this newness that confronted him. He wanted her to press him against her as she usually did, and to kiss him and promise things would be as they had always been. But the only sound that greeted him was a tree branch scraping the side of the house menacingly. The creaking of the house grew louder as if the house would fall apart, like the houses of blocks that he and Junior often built. He lay still for a long time, breathing in the unfamiliar wetness that clung to the insides of his nostrils and made him chilly.

Finally, he sat up because his diapers were wet and terribly uncomfortable. He peered through his crib's bars at the bed of Junior, who was sleeping soundly. Junior had had a fit last night and had fallen asleep late, thoroughly exhausted. Everyone had been so upset; last night, things had been terrible.

Nestor scrambled up and out the crib. Barefoot and cold, he ran out the room and down the hall and stairs. He paused by the music room. Morning light had filtered in and he could see that a window was boarded up. Rags were scattered on the floor to soak up the water that had gushed in through the window.

He glanced at the piano stool and shivered. Last night his parents had an important visitor over for dinner. To keep him and Junior out of the grownups' way, *Yaya* Taying had entertained him and Junior in the music room.

During suppertime, Nestor became fussy, and he went to Taying and asked to "titi." Taying sat on the piano stool and picked him up. She lifted her blouse to give him her breast and Nestor began suckling. Junior, who had been playing with model soldiers, saw them. He dropped his toys, joined them and said he also wanted to "titi." Taying shook her head. "You're too big, no."

Junior took a deep breath until his face turned red, and then he screamed.

"Ssshhh, don't cry! Your parents will get angry. We have an important visitor," Taying begged.

Junior howled louder, as if in agony.

Giving in, Taying gestured for Junior to come near her and she allowed the older boy to take her other breast into his mouth. For a few seconds the two boys suckled contentedly until it entered Junior's mind to pull away from Taying's nipple. Very quickly, he pointed the *yaya's* nipple toward Nestor, then he squeezed so that milk squirted all over the younger brother's face. The feel of warm milk spraying his face surprised Nestor, and he pulled away from Taying's breast. His eyes lit up when he realized what his brother was doing. Imitating his older brother, he squeezed his *yaya's* nipple. The two boys played with her breasts, as if they were playing with water pistols.

Taying was distraught but did not know what to do. She considered spanking the boys, but their cries would only get her in trouble. The best she could do was beg them to please stop, that what they were doing wasn't nice.

Disregarding her weak pleas, the boys kept up the game, that is until the visitor, who was the Chairman of the Board of Ubec's Electric Company, wandered into the music room from the living room, paused in front of the three and bellowed: "What have you here, Jose? Two calves?"

Jose Hernandez, who had been smoking his pipe in the living room, got up to investigate. Even though Taying had pulled her blouse down, he got enough of the picture to understand what had gone on. He gave the two boys two hard swats on their bottoms and exiled them to the kitchen.

April soon appeared in the kitchen, whitefaced, livid. She had tried hard to impress their visitor; she had used her Wedgewood China, her sterling service; she had culled up all her Manila sophistication, and here her two boys and their *yaya* made them appear like provincial hicks, something she had wanted desperately to avoid.

She took it out on Taying. "What do you think you were doing, right in front of our visitor? Don't you know better than to nurse those two boys in public, like lowclass people, that's what it looks like, just like those ignorant women breast-feeding their babies in buses? And besides, these boys are too old to be breast-feeding; don't you know any better than to wean them once and for all? I didn't hire you just to sit around doing nothing. You're supposed to take care of those children!"

"I have been trying, señora, but the boys cry."

"Well, do something about it or else you'll have to leave!" April shouted.

That was what had happened last night, and this cold, early morning, he hurried to the dirty kitchen to look for *Yaya* Taying. He wanted to erase last night, to make everything all right once again.

His head barely touched the top of the rough-hewn table. He looked up and around the room. Two maids scampered here and there, shutting all the windows and doors from the heavy rain. The cook was bent over the hearth, digging out yesterday's burning embers from under the ashes, then blowing back life to them. Very carefully, she piled crumpled paper and firewood on top of the glowing embers. He continued scanning the room until at last he spotted Taying. She was there; she had not left after all. She was standing in front of an ironing board, pressing an enormous, billowy white sheet. He chortled.

Upon hearing him, everyone paused and the cook said: "Why are you walking around barefoot? You'll get worms." She whisked him up and carried him to where his *Yaya* Taying was.

Yaya Taying did not smile as he expected her to; she simply placed the iron down and lifted him.

"You're awake," she said, holding him up to scrutinize him. "And wet. Come, let's change you." Unceremoniously, she plopped him down on the bench and proceeded to change his diaper.

He tugged at her skirt, wanting for her to lift her blouse and offer him her breast. Instead, she shook her head. "I'll fix you milk."

She went to the cupboard and took out a can of Carnation evaporated milk. She opened this, poured half the can into an enamel cup, then added water. She stirred in sugar, and offered him the cup. He sipped the milk, felt the thick liquid coat his throat, and he swallowed hard its strong flavor.

"It's good for you. It will make you grow big and strong, just like a Carnation Baby." She pointed at a calendar on the wall with the picture of a fat smiling baby. Sighing in resignation, he drank the rest of the milk. Maybe it would wash away last night.

The memory of last night continued to hover around, even when Taying placed him on the bench near the rough-hewn table and he watched her chop and mince vegetables on a block of wood. "When the fire is lit, Lena will fix you and Junior your oatmeal. This is for lunch. You'll also have liver. I'll chop it up, add ketchup if necessary. It's big-boy food," she said.

She did not sound happy, and so he sat quietly, somberly.

Taying was a woman in her mid-twenties. She was small in build, with a round face and two deep dimples on her cheeks. Her long hair was anchored at her nape with a tortoise-shell comb. She had a quiet, pleasant demeanor, and even when Junior hit her during his tantrums, she would calmly say, "No, Junior, don't hurt people."

She was the mother of Carding, who was two years older than Junior. She had been hired as Junior's wet-nurse shortly after April gave birth to Junior, and she had breastfed Carding and Junior simultaneously. When Nestor was born, Taying weaned Carding, so she could continue breast-feeding her employer's two children — Junior and Nestor. For all practical purposes, she served as the boys' mother. In many ways, she was closer to them than to her own son, Carding, who had been dispatched to her hometown of Lozada to be raised by her mother after he was weaned and it became impossible for Taying to take care of three boys.

Nestor sat observing the woman who was closest to him, while outside the rain slanted down, and the tall trees strained against the winds. He had the sensation that the world had changed, and the sun would never shine again. It would rain forever. He hated rain then, hated all that water that washed out of the sky, hated how it seeped into the house no matter how carefully they bolted all windows and doors, hated the smell of mushrooms that wafted from damp corners of the house.

Junior was in a terrible mood when he woke up. He flung the bowl of oatmeal that the cook gave them. When Taying told him he would have to stay in the kitchen until he ate, Junior threw himself backwards from the bench and fell head first on the concrete floor. Junior's crying was interrupted by Jose's appearance in the kitchen. Without saying anything, he picked up Junior from the floor and spanked him. Junior's loud crying dissolved into soft sobbing, which persisted even when Taying fed the two boys one spoonful at a time.

The storm worsened as the day went on, and it grew darker indoors so that the servants lit some candles. They were jittery, anxious. They talked about roads flooding and bridges being washed away. And there was a man, they said, whose head was cut off by a corrugated metal sheet zipping through the air

The sense of doom rooted in the child-Nestor, and he became quiet, as if withdrawing to another world, as if dislocated from people's hysteria, and the lightning flashing in the sky and torrents of rain falling on the roof.

It became worse at nighttime. Nestor had been dreading it most of all, even before Taying changed them into their pajamas. He had clung to the hope that this night would be like any other night, that Taying would lay down with both boys on Junior's bed. She would bare her breast to Nestor and she would pat both their backs until the boys fell asleep. But now, she simply tucked them in, checked the windows and left. Nestor could not hold himself back and started sobbing. Junior, who had been crying all day and who was exhausted, rooted around in his bed, then fell asleep. For a long time Nestor lay still, looking at the wild shadows on the walls and ceiling. It was cold; it was frightening; and he was all alone. He felt the darkness, felt as if he were sinking into a deep, deep pit. Then, when it seemed almost unbearable, the door opened slightly so that candlelight sprayed into the room. He heard footsteps, then arms lifted him out of the crib. It was Taying. He began to sob uncontrollably. She set the candle down and sat on the rocking chair with him in her arms. "Sshhh," she said, lifting her blouse to offer him her breast. "Stop your crying, I'm here." Her right hand stroked his hair.

He nuzzled his head against her breast and surrendered to the sensation of warm milk filling his mouth. With his thumb and forefinger, he played with the silky hair of her armpits. The feeling of lightness, of traveling upward from the dark pit spread over him. Most important, he felt the dreaded memory of last night dissolving in his *Yaya* Taying's warm, smoky scent. Everything was all right once again.

Holy Week
(1926)

Nestor Hernandez's older brother, Junior, cooked up the idea of going to the mines. Jose Junior, called Junior by his family and friends, was eighteen, two years older than Nestor, and more brash. The two brothers and their friend, Mario Cepeda, had been shooting baskets. It was the afternoon of Good Friday, a time when townsfolk either stayed home or went to church. People believed that during the celebration of Christ's death, Satan and his malevolent spirits ruled, which was why they avoided calling attention to themselves. People also behaved as if indeed someone they knew personally had died. They prayed; they pondered on the biblical account of Jesus' death. Even outside church, they spoke in whispers, and the entire day had a somberness and seriousness unlike any other. Early in the morning and throughout the day, the chanting of the *Pasion* recounting Jesus' *Seven Last Words* could be heard over every transistor radio in town.

Mario Cepeda, who came from the coastal town of Santander, had arrived the day before to spend Easter weekend in Mantalongon with the Hernandez family. In fact, the real reason he was in the mountain town was to visit Sofia Delgado. Sofia, seventeen and quite pretty, had the added advantage of being a good cook, an attribute — people mistakenly predicted — that would land her a husband when she grew older.

Before leaving for the mines, the father of Junior and Nestor, Jose Hernandez, had instructed them to go to church or to remain quiet because it was not a safe time to be moving about, especially not at three in the afternoon, the time of Christ's death. It didn't matter that Jose himself was going to work that day, he still nagged his boys.

After Jose left, the Hernandez brothers argued with their mother, saying they didn't want to sit at home or the stuffy church. The mother, who had grown up in a Chinese household that was more Buddhist than Christian, allowed her sons to do as they pleased.

They played basketball. Mario, the tallest of the three, was scoring more than the Hernandez brothers. An easy-going type, Mario thought nothing of the matter, but Junior, who inherited his father's competitive spirit was getting peeved. "This sun is impossible. Let's go to Number 6," he suggested "It's cooler down there."

"I can't," Mario said. "I promised Sofia I'd stop by this afternoon."

The brothers glanced at each other and snickered.

"Are you henpecked by your *inamorata*? Visit her later on," Junior said.

Mario paused. "I don't know. I promised her I'd be there by three."

"Be under-the-*saya* then," sassed Junior.

Under-the-*saya* meant being under the control of a woman. "Okay then, but just for a short while," relented Mario.

The mine shafts were numbered to identify their locations: Number 1, Number 2, and so on. Number 6 was an abandoned mine shaft. Once the most productive, this particular mine shaft had suddenly dried up, and no matter how hard Jose Hernandez tried to find the coal vein, he could not. Ordinarily, Jose had an instinct for where coal could be found. Like a diviner, he would scan the mountains, valleys, and rivers of Mantalongon. After studying the terrain, he would single out several areas. He would pick up soil and rock samples; sometimes he would even eat the soil. He would sleep on the matter, sometimes dream about it. Using these methods, he would instruct his men where to dig. They almost always found coal in these areas, and the best coal at that, bituminous coal and anthracite, not lignite the lowest ranking coal.

But shaft Number 6 was another matter. Once it had dried up, Jose had found it impossible to locate the connecting seam of the coal. A geological upheaval 230 millions of years ago had shifted the layers of rock, soil, and coal underneath the earth. The layer of coal was around someplace, but it had become costly to find it, especially when there were other productive mines; and Jose had ordered his men to seal the opening and place "no trespassing" signs around the area. Mine shafts went deep into the earth and were extremely dangerous.

Under the sweltering summer sun, the Hernandez brothers and Mario Cepeda headed for Number 6. The place was so overrun with bushes and tall grasses, the boys had difficulty finding the mine entrance. They pushed aside the wild growth until they found the boards, and the Hernandez brothers plied them open. A gust of musty air blew at them, and apprehension gripped the boys' hearts. They knew the superstitions about Good Friday; they were well aware they should not be playing there. The Hernandez brothers had heard of miners falling down vertical shafts; they had heard of beams giving way and mines caving in on workers. They knew of underground explosions due to build-up of coal dust and methane gas. They had witnessed heart-wrenching moments of men digging caved-in mines for fellow-miners, only to discover they had died of suffocation. They knew all these things and yet they were drawn to Number 6 as if Destiny itself had summoned them.

The brothers were pondering, having second thoughts about their expedition when a snake slithered out of the mine opening. The three jumped back. The snake, young and skittish, was equally afraid, and it quickly disappeared into the brush. The boys laughed nervously. They tried to recover their composure. Junior, the shortest of the three and who compensated by being the most macho, was embarrassed at his behavior. To cover-up, he turned around and blamed the others. "What sissies you two are. You're like the *bayots* sashaying up and down Remedios Boulevard."

"I'm not a sissy," Nestor said. "You're the sissy. You were about to run away."

"I did not! You were the one who turned pale, all because of that little snake. Why, it was no bigger than a tapeworm."

"You're such a sissy, you're probably scared to go down, afraid you'll come across some other little snake," Nestor retorted.

"I'm not afraid."

"Are too."

"Am not."

"Are."

"Not."

"So prove you're not afraid," Nestor dared his older brother. "Go down."

"Fine," Junior said. "I'll go down if both of you go down."

"Sure," Nestor said, without second thought.

Mario got down on his knee, and grasping the edge of the mine entrance, he studied the coconut timber supporting the shaft. He stared at the wooden steps built against one side of the shaft. The steps, which were narrow strips of wood, disappeared into the dark earth. He had the sensation of staring down an endless tunnel that plunged deep into the bowels of the earth. For a split second he wondered where it led to, what it was like down there. The pit of his stomach quivered. His parents had told him never to go down the mine shafts, ever. The Cepeda family had always been seafarers and they understood the sea. Mario's father, the Mayor of Santander, could tell from the color of the sea how deep the water was. He could tell from the way the birds skittered about when a typhoon was coming. He could hold up his forefinger and wave it around to determine the moisture in the air and he could tell from the way the breeze blew when and where the typhoon would blow in. Fish, seaweed, crabs, shrimps, seashells, sea urchins, sea cucumbers, everything related to the sea, the Cepedas understood. But matters of geology — mountains, rocks, soil — the kind of things the Hernandezes knew by second nature, the Cepedas knew little about. Mario literally felt like fish plucked out of the water. If he had a choice, he would rather be with Sofia at the moment. That prospect seemed far more pleasant. Sofia would have a pitcher of cold *calamansi* juice ready; she would have home-made rice cakes; and they would sit on the verandah and catch the afternoon breeze while they joked, and gossiped, and professed their love for each other.

Junior sensed that Mario wanted to leave, and went on the attack. "Well then, who's the sissy?"

"It's like a ladder, that's all," Nestor said, trying to assure Mario. "Just hang on to the sides and use the steps."

"It's well . . . so dark," Mario said, "and deep. What if there are bats in there or snakes." He shivered.

"We know snakes live there," Junior said. "We saw how that little one scared you. Come on, if you can jump to shoot baskets, you can go down Number 6."

His *amor proprio* pricked, Mario stood up and said, "Fine, you go down first."

Junior, who was being groomed by his father to run the coal mines one day and who grew up scampering in and out of these mine shafts, clambered down the shaft, and was soon up. He stared at Mario triumphantly. Mario shook his head. "You go next, Nestor."

Nestor, agile and sure-footed, who considered the coal mines an extension of his home, went down and climbed up, as if he were going up and down regular house stairs.

It was Mario's turn. Mario, who swam before he walked, was terrified. Once he had dreamt of an earthquake and the earth opened up and he fell into a crack that closed up over him. Ever since, he had a fear of confined spaces. He wanted to tell the Hernandez brothers his dream and explain to them why he couldn't go down, but he couldn't find the words to express his fear. Besides the two Hernandez brothers had little smirks on their faces, and their mocking him weighed heavier than his fear. He took a deep breath and started to climb down. He did so very carefully, placing one foot down before lowering the other, hugging the split coconut logs that served as railings. He did not look down; he went by feel, relying on when his feet touched the lower step. Down he descended where the air turned cooler and thinner. Soon, it became pitch-black, and the only light was the circle of brightness above him, a beacon that became smaller and smaller the farther down he descended. "How far down should I go?" he shouted, his words echoing around him.

"Just keep on going," Junior shouted back.

"Let him come up," Nestor reasoned with his brother.

"He needs to finish what he started. You know how Papa insists that we finish what we're doing. Let him." And to Mario, he shouted, "When you see the white handkerchief, you can come back up."

"I can't see a thing."

"It's white, you can't miss it. It's tied to the right side."

Mario looked down and saw blackness. He twisted his body and turned his head. He saw it! A quick flicker of white, like St. Elmo's fire, and triumphantly he yelled, "I found it!"

"Well, come on up then. You better hurry, Sofia will be waiting for you," Junior said. "Invite us over for *merienda* will you? I'm sure Sofia cooked something for you. Maybe she's made you soup from bull testicles. That'll make you wild for her." Junior laughed.

Mario detested being teased about Sofia. He started climbing; he wanted to get hold of Junior and punch him. Sofia was the girl he loved, and her name shouldn't be bandied about like that. Mario moved quickly, but in his haste, he became reckless and missed a step. He lost his balance and fell. He screamed, and at first the Hernandez boys laughed because Mario was proving himself a sissy; but when silence followed, they became frightened.

The boys fretted by the mine shaft, pacing back and forth, wondering what to do. It wasn't only Mario's accident that upset them so, it was fear of their father who never hesitated whipping them with his leather belt. Nestor finally insisted they report the incident. They ran to their father's office. Faces white from fright, they confessed that Mario fell down Number 6. "What do you mean?" bellowed Jose. Bit by bit, the boys gave a version of the accident that laid the blame on Mario.

"That foolish boy," Jose declared, "He's fit only to be a fisherman." He ordered his best men to climb down Number 6 to recover Mario's body.

The incident shook Mantalongon. It was not unusual for miners to die at the mines, but Mario was the son of a politician. Jose Hernandez anticipated the question of blame and he instructed his two sons to say it was Mario who wanted to go down the mine shaft. The parents of Mario insisted that this was untrue because they had known about his earthquake dream. But the brothers were steadfast and convincing: the three of them had been happily playing basketball, when it had entered Mario's mind to go to the mine shaft. The brothers had warned him that it was dangerous, but Mario was adamant. He had even wanted to go to Number 6 alone; the brothers had no choice but to accompany him. Despite their protests, Mario had gone down and the dreadful accident had happened. Nestor repeated this tale to the chief of police; Junior wept when he gave his report.

So convincing were the Hernandez brothers, that even Mario's parents wavered and wondered if some demon had possessed Mario to make him instigate the whole incident; it was Good Friday after all.

When they saw Mario's mangled body, they regained their equilibrium, and the father wanted to bring the matter to court. His friends pointed out that Jose Hernandez was wealthy and could pay off judges. The matter could drag on for years. The father considered quicker justice by sending his men with guns to Mantalongon to have a shoot-out with the miners of Jose Hernandez, but Mario's mother reasoned with her husband that no matter how many people they killed, her son would still be dead. She begged him to lift the matter up to God and try to move on on with their lives.

The drama did not end there. Mario's body was such a terrible sight, his parents ordered the casket closed. They went ahead and had a three-day wake, which left the mourners disconcerted since they were used to having an open casket with the corpse in full view while they ate, talked, and gambled at the funeral parlor. Sofia Delgado traveled to Santander to see Mario for the last time. She was feeling particularly guilty because she had been very angry at Mario Cepeda for standing her up on Good Friday. She had made quite a scene at her house, saying she would never see him again and that she wished he were dead. When she had learned that Mario had indeed died, she bit her tongue and cursed herself. Without speaking to anyone, she had locked herself in a bedroom where she cut off her long hair. Holy Saturday, she had talked her sister Bianca into accompanying her to Santander. The girls had risen at dawn and traveled for eight hours. Dusty and tired they appeared at the Mortuario de San Jose where they found Mario's family and their friends in the rear section of the chapel. Mario's casket was in front of the altar, but the lid was closed. Without greeting anyone, Sofia went to the casket and started to open it. The funeral director rushed forward to stop Sofia, and he explained that the casket had to be closed. Crying, Sofia begged the parents to allow her to see Mario's body for the last time. The father was adamant, he did not want anyone seeing his son looking like something that had gone through the meat grinder. When Mario's mother saw Sofia pale, frightened, and completely distraught, she understood that this girl loved her son, and she allowed her to peek into the casket. Sofia, whose imagination had been raging from the moment she received the bad news, was somewhat relieved to find Mario recognizable. He had black-and-blue marks on his face; half his face was swollen; his neck had clearly been broken; and most amazing of all was that Mario looked very old and tired.

Sofia did not sleep for three nights. On the fourth night, she had her first "falling dream," a dream that would recur for the rest of her life. The dream had several versions, but the basic facts consisted of Sofia walking along a mountain trail. The trail suddenly ended, and she found herself stepping off into thin air. She fluttered down slowly, like a dry leaf, but when she reached the ground, she hit it with such violence that she could feel her skull splitting, her bones cracking, her heart thundering within her; and she awoke with a jolt. Sofia never wore colorful clothes again; and she never loved another man. It was too much trouble, she would respond in jest, when pressed about the matter.

When summer vacation ended and school resumed, Jose Hernandez quickly dispatched his two sons to Manila schools. Out of sight, out of mind, he figured, hoping the scandal would die down. By this time, Jose Hernandez was a very wealthy man who had developed a ruthless streak. He had taken his resources and his Chinese wife's dowry, and made each centavo grow a thousand-fold. Aside from manipulating documents so he could acquire all the mines of the area, he underpaid his workers.

Following the style of *haciendaros*, he kept a store in his mining camp and there being no other store in the area, his workers bought his overpriced food and goods. His workers ran up credit to buy their necessities, and their next month's salary barely paid what they owed at the store. It was almost like slavery.

There was still another repercussion regarding Mario's death. Sometime after his death when the Hernandez boys were already in Manila, and when life had gained a semblance of normalcy, a miner from Baguio joined the camp. His name was Juan Bautista, and he had visited America briefly where he picked up the notion of organizing a labor union. Looking for an emotional issue as a focal point, Juan Bautista resuscitated Mario's death and made a political matter out of it. He talked about the poor work conditions at the mines; he talked about child labor; he talked about the rampant silicosis and tuberculosis among miners and their families; he talked about the high mortality rate at the Hernandez mines. Jose, not one to hem-and-haw where money was concerned, ordered his foreman to get rid of the mastermind of the budding labor union. Soon after, Juan Bautista was found dead at the bottom of Number 6, and since he was not the son of a politician but was a poor miner from Baguio, his body was shipped to his relatives without fanfare, and there the matter ended.

Meanwhile, the brothers found themselves in Manila, with clean slates so to speak, because Manileños didn't have the foggiest notion where Mantalongon was. They didn't even know if Mantalongon was a place or a vegetable. Jose Junior threw himself into his studies — engineering — and it was a struggle for him, because his brain stopped understanding math with trigonometry. As his father's heir-apparent however, he worked hard to get the rudiments of engineering down. He would eventually assist his father in running the mines, and one day he would kill himself by throwing himself down another mine shaft.

Nestor, who was in his last year of high school, occasionally thought about Mario's death. He tempered his guilt by hanging on to the thought that it had been Junior who had egged on Mario. Even though he had liked Mario and felt sorry for what had happened to him, Nestor thought Mario had been pretty dumb about the whole matter. Risking his life to save face was stupid. This was one lesson Nestor learned from the tragic incident. In addition, he picked up the idea that if you lie and stick with your lie, you can convince some people that your lie is the truth, or at the very least you can confuse them about the issue.

There was still another lesson that seeped into his brain, not as a conscious thought but as a wordless impression that he picked up observing his father's handling of the tragedy: money can buy intangible things like freedom, respect, credibility, and most important of all, power. This last lesson would dominate his life. Because of it, he would give up the woman he truly loved, and like his father and older brother would settle for a wealthy Chinese woman whom he did not really love; and he would spend more than half his life as a rich but miserable man.

Killing the Lamb

Speech slurred, Cora shouted that he drank too much; and so in front of her and his mother, Nestor held up the bottle of Scotch so it caught the morning sunlight, scattered shards of rainbow in the dining room. He slowly poured himself a drink. With glazed eyes, April turned away and continued giving instructions to the cook. April had the ability to ignore such matters. Years ago, April had not noticed the sharp words and beatings Nestor's father had given Nestor and Junior. It was an ability that Nestor sometimes wished he had. He, on the contrary, perceived things that gnaw, that upset his bones, that drove him to doing exactly this sort of thing, drinking early in the morning. He was a doctor; he knew this was not good for him; and yet, two glasses cut the sting of things, made the prospect of a long day tolerable.

In Manila, he didn't drink as much, just the usual social drinking, very acceptable. As Mininster of Health he had been preoccupied with meetings, making decisions, greasing palms, getting his palms greased, making money, and there was a lot to be made. It made the time pass: up at six in the morning, and out of the house before eight, before Cora was awake, meetings throughout the day, and there was lunch, *merienda*, and dinner. By the time he got home, Cora was in bed. The two of them would go for days not seeing each other. It was not such a bad arrangement, considering.

But his current situation in Mantalongon was madness. Two women who quarreled with him, who quarreled with each other, who shouted at the servants, Cora in her wheelchair, April with her cane, and from their mouths leapt constant accusations of things or money lost or misplaced, food not cooked properly, the bed not done properly, the floors not swept carefully. A whirlwind of exhausting nonstop bickering. The only time he could rest was when he locked himself in his office or if he went downtown or traveled to the city, which he did as often as he could.

Even before he had joined them for breakfast, the two women had started. April had told the maid to prepare a cup of tea for Cora. "It's good for you, Cora. It's better than coffee."

Cora glared at her mother-in-law. "If I want tea, I'll ask for it!"

"Cora, if you had listened to me in the first place, you wouldn't be in the situation you're in. I told you years ago to change your diet, that pork and rich food were bad for you. You never listened, now see what has happened. This stroke could have been prevented. Even the doctor said so. Diet and exercise, he said. I have been saying the same thing for years. I eat plenty of fish and vegetables, and people mistake me for sixty. Look at me, an old woman like myself passing for sixty. Your household had nothing but fried foods; and your cook used pork lard at that, I'm surprised Nestor hasn't gotten sick as you have."

"Nestor, tell your mother to stop!"

Nestor turned away from them, thinking how tiresome they both were, but Cora more so because at least his mother was his kin whereas Cora had boiled down to nothing more than an obligation. They were simply stuck with each other. They did not share love, nor laughter, nor joy, nor peace. They shared houses, things, cars, and a constant simmering dislike for each other. During key points of his life he'd looked at himself and realized he was no saint, and he had accepted Cora's stroke and move to Mantalongon as punishment from God.

Both women watched him, waiting for him to take sides.

He picked up his glass of Scotch. "I'm going to my office."

They continued staring, Cora with a look of hatred, and his mother with an expression that said he had betrayed her. In retaliation, his mother barked at him: "Nestor, don't forget to sort out your father's trunk. Your father kept important papers there and it's high time you go through those papers. Don't ignore me, I am your mother."

In his office, with the door bolted behind him, he sat down and sipped his Scotch, feeling the cool drink slip down this throat, then miraculously warming him, reminding him he was still alive. He closed his eyes, thinking Manila was much better, with his huge house and busy schedule.

He pressed his hands to his forehead, felt a tightening deep within his brain, then decided he should snap out of it, do something, or else he'd lose it, go raving mad, like Junior who just couldn't take it, and who checked out of all this. He opened his eyes and caught sight of the pile of mail. He should at least look at bank statements and make sure his portfolio was in good shape, but movement outside the window caught his attention. It was a blur of white against the green grass. A cloud of soft white against rolling green hills — the sheep were grazing in the field.

The sheep were his father's idea — his father's caprice, more precisely. There are around fifty of them now; his father had started with only six. Five years before he died, Jose Hernandez had visited Australia for an ASEAN energy conference where he got the idea to raise sheep. He hired a shepherd and a vet for the animals. Jose had doted on the sheep, providing them with a special shed, all the vitamins they needed. From six animals, the herd grew to fifty. There were a smattering of black sheep and around half-a-dozen newly born lambs. The first time Nestor had seen his father with his sheep, he had been surprised at how softly he spoke to the sheep, and how carefully he tended to their needs. Jose never treated him and Junior as gently. Nestor had been irritated, and he had stayed away from Mantalongon, but later, as Minister of Health, he did have to visit Mantalongon occasionally. By this time, Junior was dead, and Nestor could see that despite Jose's hard shield, Junior's death had taken its toll on him. Jose had grown gray and forgetful; and instead of fighting with the other mine owners as he liked to do, he passed the time at home with his sheep.

Nestor watched the newborn lambs scampering after their mothers. The mothers paused occasionally so the young ones could nurse, then they moved on, with the young ones racing alongside. He observed a young one that kept falling down. It had white curly fur; it was a pretty one. The mother nudged it to get up; the lamb tried to get up but its legs were weak, and it toppled down. This went on for a while, and Nestor considered calling the shepherd to ask about the newborn, but he knew the shepherd would tell him it was a runt. The shepherd would pick up the lamb and take it to its mother. He would set it on its feet, but it would fall down. Eventually, he would give the newborn a bottle, but tomorrow, when Nestor would ask about the lamb, the shepherd would say it died. He would say, "It's that way when there are too many of them."

He downed his drink. What was the point? It was all quite hopeless, futile. You ask, you make the emotional investment, you single out this one animal, and the animal dies. It had been that way at medical school; you singled out a patient, grew attached them, cared for them, and then they died. A long time ago, he had been the doctor to a ten-year-old girl who had cancer. When he first saw her, her eyes were large and bright, and she managed to mask her fear behind her cheerfulness. She had taken it upon herself to take care of the younger ones in her ward. He would catch her reading or singing to the younger patients. And he had felt it, that invisible thread linking him to the girl; he could feel his spirit lift when he saw her smiling face. He had tried his best to save her; he had exhausted all his knowledge, consulted other doctors, sent for medication from the States; but like the rest of them, she shrank until she became a pile of bones and her hair fell off and she looked like a strange bird, and then she died. So what was the point?

He looked around the large room filled with books, ledgers, trophies, plaques, and pictures. These were accumulations of symbols of success of his father and himself. And yet neither he nor his father had been happy. So, really, what was the point?

Nestor decided to make it easy for the lamb and for everyone. He would tell the shepherd to kill it today, cut off its head, gut it, and make stew from its meat. That would simplify matters.

He itched for another drink, but stopped himself because he didn't want to go to the bar and run into Cora or his mother again. That deep tightening in his head started once again. He picked up his glass and rolled the cool sides of it on his forehead. It was really more than a drink he hankered for, but what he wanted was like a phantom. He wanted something that had escaped him, something that could no longer be. Once, he dreamed of a life unlike his current life, a life that was in fact pronouncedly the opposite of his life now. Luisa had been part of that dream. But he lost that dream, and in its place were Cora and his mother yelling at each other upstairs. In place of the gilded dreams he had once painted, was a lifetime of tiresome days, meaningless, pointless — he was at the end of his rope; that was how he felt before he called the shepherd to order him to kill the lamb.

Juana La Guapa

Dear Luisa,

At the river, you asked me to leave you alone. I know I should. I have tried to do just that. Years ago, when I learned you were carrying Fermin's child, I willed myself to stay away from you. It was not easy to do. That single night in Maibog has stretched into timeless eternity; a part of me remains lost back there. When I heard about your pregnancy, then the birth of your daughter, I vowed to leave you alone. For decades I did, but now, you are back once again and it is the thought of you that will not leave me alone. I should let you go, release you, because you have found peace, whereas I, on the other hand, wallow in purgatory.

We thought my parents hated you and your family and therefore they separated us. We had agreed that the whole thing had been arranged, orchestrated, that our lives had been manipulated, that we were pawns. That much you had figured out; and Papa had told me pretty much the same thing on his death bed. He was sorry, he said, for what he did to us.

Let me write down everything, Luisa. Let me write it down so I can hold the matter up and turn it around and study it from every angle, understand it from every perspective, absorb the truth into every single cell of my body.

Papa looked terrible before he died. He was emaciated, a pile of bones; his skin had a bluish-black cast; he had difficulty breathing. He had smoked most of his life and in his raspy voice, he had asked me to sit by him on his bed. I did so awkwardly. I felt like a nervous child, instead of the Important Man I thought I had become. I held his hand, cold and bony. My mother was there, and also his nurse; but he sent them out of the room. He started crying. I had never seen my father cry, not even when Junior died. I thought he was afraid of dying and I tried to cheer him up, saying he'd get well soon.

"I'll die," he said. "This heart will go. Heart attacks, Nestor, many of the Hernandez men die of heart attacks. Don't smoke. And I hear you drink too much. You're a doctor, you should know better. Give that up."

He started coughing. It was a loose cough; I could picture his lungs like mush. I patted his back.

"I'll be all right, Pa. Don't strain yourself."

He took deep breaths until he gained control, then said: "I need to speak to you."

My father had never needed anything.

He sounded very serious and I didn't know what to say, how to behave.

For years I had hated him, now I was afraid to lose him. I had been on my own for so long and had not needed him nor my mother, but at that moment the cold chill of fear ran up my spine. I thought of the time he spent at the coal mines, away from us. He had always been too busy, and on many occasions he had been cruel to my mother and to Junior and myself; and yet here I hankered for him. I yearned for his love, for his approval; I longed for an idyllic past with him that could never be. He pulled his hand away from mine and reached up to stroke my forehead, a gesture I was unaccustomed to. I was surprised at his touch; it made me weep.

"Nestor, be careful of Carding. He has been my right-hand man but it doesn't mean he can be trusted. He will try to take advantage of you when I am gone. He has been a good runner and fixer, but he could easily turn against you, so check the books carefully and don't give him too many liberties. Do not ever give him free rein of deposits and withdrawals. Make sure there's someone who'll check on him."

"Don't think about those things," I muttered, "everything will be all right. The important thing is that you get well."

"I'm not going to get better. Let's not fool ourselves. I've worked too hard to build up the mines; it's taken me a lifetime, it would be a shame to let it go down the drain. You must take over."

"Yes, Pa. Don't worry."

"Promise me!" he insisted. He was clawing at my arm.

"I promise."

He relaxed, lay back and his expression softened. "How are things? Is the president taking care of you? Do you know his wife lived in Ubec and was Carnival Queen? She does not look much like a beauty queen, but money talks. I knew her parents well. How is it to be Minister of Health?" he asked, then started laughing, coughing as he did so. When he caught his breath, he said, "Imagine the irony, me the way I am, you the Minister of Health."

My sorrow turned into a lump in my throat. I swallowed my sorrow, composed myself. "I've been very busy. A lot of political functions. And a lot of in-fighting, you have to constantly watch your back."

"I'm sure you can handle it. I'm proud of you." He paused then asked, "And Cora?"

"She was busy, Pa. She wanted to come, but couldn't. She sends her love —"

He waved his hand to stop me. "Nestor, there is no need to pretend. I understand everything. I am sorry for you. Come closer, look at you.

Everyone can see the strain on your face. And don't tell me it's because of work. I know better."

He sighed and was quiet for a long time, then he continued, "I have never discussed it, but it's time to do so. Your mother and I believed Cora would make a good match. It was one of the rare moments your mother and I agreed on something. It's true that Cora's family connections have helped you, but your unhappiness is written all over you. I have seen her scream and have a fit at the servants and even at you."

"Cora is always nervous and always expects the worst."

"You don't have to protect that woman. Your marriage has been a disaster. I'm sorry. I should have spoken to you; I should have advised you to marry the woman you loved. Money you can earn; power you can acquire; but love is something else. It's a gift. You have probably figured out by now that your mother and I did not love each other. We learned to get along. She stayed out of my way; she ran the household, raised you kids. But love? It wasn't there. It had never been there. From the start we understood each other. A marriage, you see, doesn't have to be out of love. After all, love passes. Marriage is a contract, an agreement between two people, and as long as you see eye-to-eye, well then, that's fine. But you and Cora never saw eye-to-eye. I know you have never forgotten Luisa. Luisa was a good girl. Your mother and I had nothing personal against her, but she was a Delgado."

He stopped, as if allowing me to digest that last sentence.

I made no reaction and he went on, "There's always been bad blood between the Delgados and our family. Her father and I had disagreements over mining claims here in Mantalongon. He was my stepfather's nephew, so there were some ties there. Since he didn't follow the matter up in court, I took over his claims." He started to get agitated. I patted his back.

"I paid some people, had some papers changed. He could have challenged me; he had the right, but he didn't care. He was a poet, very irresponsible."

"It was something the courts decided, don't worry about it," I said.

"I need to talk to Luisa, Nestor. I need to tell her the truth. The truth — it's now the time for truth, isn't it? I need to confess. I must tell her what I have never been able to tell another. The truth — I want to tell the truth — find her and tell her I need to see her, Nestor.

"Listen to me because these are the words of a dying man. I need to confess, not to a priest. Do you know those people are such damn hypocrites? They eat rich food; they bed their laundrywomen; and yet they dare tell people what to do. They are men, all the same, sinful men like you and me

"I need to confess that I have sinned — against you, against your mother, against your brother, against many people. I have sinned, and because of my sins I have been punished. It was no coincidence that your brother took his life at the mines — do not protest. He did not fall down accidently, he committed suicide. Your mother wants to pretend it was an accident; it is easier for her to swallow this than the truth. Let her live in her fantasies; the older she gets the more like her own mother she becomes — that fat old woman who lived in her own world. Your grandmother talked of nothing but Canton, Canton all the time, as if it were the center of the universe; she had forgotten what poor farmfolk she came from. Maybe I'm no better. Perhaps I have filled my mind with dreams; perhaps that is how one survives. But it's time for the truth now, time to look at things while there is time. Your brother was miserable. I didn't see it then, but I see it now. He never had the head for this kind of business — he hated the mines; he hated his wife; he was embarrassed of his simpering son, that flaming faggot who likes young boys. I didn't understand that Junior was not made of the same stock as I am. He came from soft clay; I come from something harder.

"Did he tell you about his dreams? I have been thinking about them, wondering what they meant. In one, he was running along a narrow road and someone was chasing him. Junior never knew exactly who was chasing him, but it was something frightening, something dangerous, and so he ran as fast as he could down this narrow road. Sometimes, he would be out of breath, weary, but he couldn't stop or else he would be caught. His other dream was auditory; he dreamt of doors slamming, first one, then another, then still another. He told me these strange dreams just three weeks before he died. I should have listened carefully. I could have warned him; instead I laughed. You see, I never have anxious dreams like that. I dream of scaling mountains; I dream of swimming deep oceans.

"Junior could not take unhappiness and transform it into some other force aside from self-destruction. I have done precisely that. It is not easy to do, but you take the pain and unhappiness and twist it according to your will. You overcome it; you don't succomb to it. I was able to do it, although I still have to account to God to see if indeed I did not self-destruct all the same. Perhaps my life was simply a slower spiralling down, unlike Junior who wanted the quicker way out. What a fool, jumping down a mine shaft. What a shame. If I had understood his dreams, I could have warned him.

"Nestor, listen, because you are still young — you still have many years left — listen, so that you can learn and save yourself unlike Junior. I have been wrong. I thought I did the right thing; I believed I made the right choices; but somewhere I made a mistake. I don't know where."

He ran out of breath and had another coughing spell. When he recovered, he went on to talk about you. "Luisa has never said anything. She stays away from Mantalongon, but once I ran into her in church. She looked smart in her expensive clothes and jewelry. I could see she was well-heeled, far better off than she had been. But there was hurt in her face. Anger too. A beautiful woman in her smart clothes angry at me; obviously I was on the wrong track. Yes, I am to blame; I need her forgiveness. And Nestor, forgive me. I need your forgiveness as well."

He said these words with great difficulty. He was an old man, a dying man. My father. Even though I held a grudge against him, I told him his concerns belonged to the past, that they didn't matter any more, that things were all right, and not to worry.

I looked for you, found you by the river and asked you to see him. You declined. Shortly after, he lapsed into a coma and died.

His wake, funeral, days of prayer, and work kept me occupied. It wasn't until recently when his words returned to me, like an incessant buzzing that won't go away. It's only now that the pieces have fallen into place, like a puzzle. Another mirage shimmers. Something has come up, and I must tell you because it's your picture too, it's your life as well.

I have been on a journey for the truth.

My Yaya Taying gave her version of the truth. Like the prodigal son, I returned to her at the Jagubiao Leprosarium. Yes, she is a leper. She insisted on darkness so I would not see her face and her hands. I expected the worst but saw a shruken shadow with a veil over its face, and the shadow spoke about my past and Junior's as well as my father's and mother's past. I listened to that voice in that cocoon of darkness. After fifty-some years I could still recall her scent and stranger still, feel absolutely certain about her affection for me.

I have also uncovered letters and journals that my father wrote when he was a young man — still another version of the truth. I found these in his trunk. It is an old Chinese trunk with a dome lid made of wood and fully carved. It came from his mother. My father alone opened and locked this trunk. After his death, even my mother would not open it. I finally did.

I had always perceived my father in a certain way: he was a brusque man, a sharp businessman, a harsh husband and father. It was strange to read the writings of the young man he had been. The author of these writings was young enough to be my son. It was like meeting another person. I had never known my father to be vulnerable; I had never known him to be idealistic; I had never known him to be in love with another human being. The father I knew had worked hard to build and maintain a financial empire, no matter what the cost. This man was powerful and sure of himself. This man had a granite-heart, a man rigid in his ways, humourless, difficult, frightening in my ways. It was a revelation to meet this other person, a lovesick boy, an insecure lad, still uncertain about the direction of his life.

From my yaya's mouth and from my father's own writing, I learned another truth, a truth that has been buried for so long, it had gotten lost in so many other stories, there is a need to expose it and preserve it.

We had not known it, but my father knew your mother. He had loved her. Juana, your mother, was known as Guapa — the Beautiful — at the Asilo de Santa Clara in Manila where they first met. The Asilo de Santa Clara was an orphanage. When she was just an infant, Juana had been left on the turning cradle at the Asilo where the nuns raised her. It was customary then for unwed mothers who had no one else to turn to, to leave their babies with the nuns. There Juana grew, trained by the nuns to do embroidery and cooking and other duties that well-bred women were taught. These young women raised at the orphanages were considered a fine catch for men seeking wives: the women knew their duties; they were religious; they were faithful.

Papa and Juana met at the turn of the century, during the beginning of the American occupation — a turbulent time. The Americans had taken over where the Spaniards left off. Commodore George Dewey had betrayed the Filipino nationalists. The Americans had come to the Philippines after the sinking of the Maine in Havana and subsequent declaration of war against Spain. Dewey's orders were to prevent the Spanish squadron from leaving the Asiatic waters. To the Filipinos, Dewey had indicated America would honor the newly-formed Philippine government, but after defeating the Spain, the tone in Washington shifted — William McKinley was the American president at the time — and orders were to retain the Islands, no matter what the cost. Papa even wrote down the statement of the famous writer, Mark Twain:

"Dewey could have gone about his affairs elsewhere and left the competent Filipino army to starve out the little Spanish garrison and send it home, and the Filipino citizens to set up the form of government they might prefer and deal with the friars and their doubtful acquisitions according to Filipino ideas of fairness and justice — ideas which have since been tested and found to be of as high an order as any that prevail in Europe or America. There must be two Americas, one that sets the captive free and one that takes a once-captive's new freedom away from him and picks a quarrel with him with nothing to found on it, then kills him to get his land."

After fighting Spain for years, the Filipinos had to fight the Americans as well. The Americans, with their superior arms had the upper hand, and ultimately the Filipino army, led by General Emilio Aguinaldo, had to retreat to Northern Luzon.

One of those who accompanied Aguinaldo was a poet turned revolutionary, Papa's cousin by marriage, his stepfather's nephew to be more precise. Papa's stepfather, Don Martin, wanted to rescue this nephew, which was why he and Papa went to Luzon.

Their first stop was the Asilo de Santa Clara because the nuns supported the Filipino nationalists and knew their whereabouts. Seasick, Papa retired to the cubicle he was assigned to. Juana served him his supper in that small room with the solitary cot. They talked for a long time, and Juana spoke of not knowing who her parents were, and her imaginings as to who they were. She thought her mother came from a humble background, although she felt her father was an important man. Papa must have felt comfortable with her because he confessed to her that he was a friar's son, a fact that embarrassed him greatly and which he never discussed with us, ever. But with Juana, he discussed the matter, telling her about the pain this caused him, and his desire to make something out of himself to make up for this "defect."

From an early age, Papa wanted to prove himself. I had not realized that his drive to achieve had actually come from a feeling of lack, that is, his insecurity drove him to make money and to gain power. I saw for the first time that Papa had imposed on us his passion to succeed. It was never verbally said, but it was always there, that push to be somebody. Junior and I were like blindfolded men led to follow the steps he laid out for us. A power-monger, that was how I knew my father.

But as a young man, he sounded like other young men, enchanted by this young woman called Guapa. Juana was one of the guides assigned to take them to Isabela Province, in the North, where the nationalists were hiding. They traveled by boat, then by land, slowly making their way to the highlands of Northern Luzon. And daily, Papa and Juana grew closer, or perhaps it was Papa who grew attached to her. He wrote a description of Juana: "Her hair reaches her ankles. It is shiny and crackles as if it has life of its own. Usually, she has this twirled in a bun at her nape, anchored down with a tortoise shell studded with seed pearls. But in the evening, she releases her hair and it is like a dark mantle surrounding her. She looks like a Madonna — indeed she is far more breathtaking than any Madonna I have seen. To call her beautiful is an understatement. Her features are even and pleasant; her eyes sparkle; her skin glows. She is alive from the tip of her hair to her toes. She smiles, she laughs, her intelligence and humour manifests itself at all times. She is called Guapa for good reason."

During the time it took to travel north, Papa fell in love with Juana. Papa had it all planned: she would return with him to Mantalongon so Juana could meet his mother. After a brief engagement, they would get married.

Papa had had an unhappy childhood. He was a frayle's son, the parish priest's bastard, and that was a stigma he had to bear. His mother had been very young when she had the liaison with the parish priest. Despite her disgrace, she married a town's official who did his best to treat Papa like his own son. But Papa continued to have a chip on his shoulder; he was always garrulous, always asserting himself. But Juana seemed to tame him; he seemed softer, more agreeable, happier in short. He wanted a happy life with her.

Papa and Juana entertained plans of marriage even while they endured the rigorous trip through the towns of Santa Lucia, to Salcedo, to Cervantes, to Avangan, all the way to Palanan — the same route Aguinaldo and his men had taken. For helping the general and his army, all these towns had been severely punished by the trailing Americans. Houses and granaries had been razed. Men, even young boys, were sometimes killed by Americans.

This experience was an eye-opener to my young father who had only known the simple life in the mountains of Ubec. In his journals, he wrote at length about the idea of power, and how the Americans were clearly in the position of power. "They have superior arms; they have all the supplies they need. They do not have to scrounge around like Aguinaldo's men who have to dig for sweet potatoes to eat. The source of their power is their money. The Americans can even buy people's loyalty; we have heard they are paying the Macabebes to be their scouts. With these mercenaries helping the Americans, it's only a matter of time before they catch Aguinaldo."

He did not state it, but it was clear that my father focused then on the importance of power. The idea that money brings power was a major theme in Papa's life and one that Papa drilled in Junior's and my heads. His own life had been dedicated to making money to gain power.

But these thoughts had not yet been fully formed in my father's head as they made their way to Northern Luzon. He was in love with Juana and dreamed of raising six children with her. Perhaps the sense of danger

124

heightened their feelings for each other. They were only just one town ahead of the Americans who became more reckless and ruthless the more frustrated they became. The Americans reportedly massacred entire barrios; they were not one to garrote or torture slowly as the Spaniards did, but they were quick to shooting, in the name of democracy.

At last, in Palanan, my father's party found his stepfather's nephew with an infected leg. Apparently, while evacuating Avangan, the nationalists had had a squirmish with an American party and the nephew had been shot. His leg was festering. He was in pain; he could not walk; he was slowing everyone down. The nationalists considered leaving him behind. When my father's party arrived, Aguinaldo was relieved because the nephew could now be sent back to civilization, instead of abandoning him to a sure death in Palanan.

All the way back to Manila, Juana nursed the nephew. Instead of writing revolutionary poems about freedom and a better life, he started writing about love. He, like my father, had fallen in love with Juana. The saddest part about the whole story, at least for my father, was that Juana fell in love with the poet.

The poet was Roberto Delgado, your father, and my father never forgave him for stealing Juana from him. My father's last entry in his journal is a spare account of the wedding of Roberto and Juana:

"At six this morning, Juana got married to Roberto. I had considered leaving for Manila today, instead of tomorrow, but out of consideration to my mother and stepfather, I have decided to attend their wedding. My absence would embarrass my stepfather greatly; Roberto is his sister's son, after all. I was afraid I would not be able to go through the ordeal, but I survived. Life is interesting, when you think you cannot bear something, all you have to do is fix in your mind that it will pass, and then it is not too bad.

Juana was a few minutes late arriving in church and briefly I wondered if she would not show up. But she did. She wore a gown that the nuns at the Asilo had made for her, pure white lace and her veil was white tulle with pearls embroidered along the hem. Her hair was parted in the middle with two pearl combs on either side to keep the veil in place. Her hair fell down her back and the tulle veil barely covered her thick mass of hair. She looked happy, giddy; and her happiness was a dagger twisting my heart. I kept telling myself I must behave like a grownup, that I must wish them both well, but deep inside, I wished the church walls would collapse on them and end the whole charade. I hated her; I loved her. I wanted to possess her; it hurt to know another man would possess her that night.

Roberto appeared with that lost look of his. Pale, insipid fellow — what did she see in him? I wondered. How I wished he had been killed in Avangan. It was too bad that the Americans didn't catch him and shoot him with their Mausers. Straight through the head, or through the heart. I detest the man. One day I will destroy him.

The wedding Mass went on, followed by the reception. There was the usual 'lechon' and turkey and 'embotidos;' and people got drunk even though it was mid-day, and there were the usual dirty jokes about newly-weds, jokes I had great difficulty laughing at.

Before leaving, I saw Juana. She kissed me on the cheek and wished me well. She asked if I had forgiven her. It was difficult to be cruel to her even though in my heart I wanted to destroy her, to destroy them both. I lied: 'What is there to forgive?' 'Thank you,' she said, 'for understanding.' She is beautiful but foolish; but what does it matter, tomorrow I will be gone."

This is the new truth Luisa, one we had never known, nor imagined. We had believed only four people counted: you, me, Fermin, and Cora. But now others are in the picture: Juana, Jose, and Roberto. This revelation will not change reality, but perhaps it will help me stop blaming myself for what happened to us, knowing there were other forces that had taken part in shaping our lives.

For the rest of my life I will carry the pain that my father could not forgive your mother, and that in fact he turned his love for her into hate not only for her but for her entire family, including you. He was sorry, Luisa. For my part, I will try to forgive him. But this rage — I do not know what to do with it; perhaps time will take care of it. People talk about time healing all wounds. and yes, once upon a time, I had believed that time would make me forget you; but they were wrong; I continue to love you still.

Love forever,
Nestor

Talking About the Woman in Cholon

Nathan wanted to see Magdalena before leaving. He drove to the child care center, bringing with him a small package, his birthday gift for her. He found her seated on a rocking chair, holding a baby in her arms.

He watched quietly by the nursery's doorway. Sunshine was streaming through the open window and a bit of light hit the back of her hair so it shone like ebony. She was playing with the baby. It was a pleasant scene and it evoked happiness in him. More than that it culled up deep feelings of longing to be with her always.

He did not call her; he took in the sight of her whispering nonsensical words to the infant, telling him how sweet he was, sweeter than cane sugar, sweet enough to eat. The baby gurgled and reached up to touch Magdalena's nose. Magdalena pretended to bite the baby's fingers; the baby laughed. Magdalena laughed, throwing her head back, and then she saw him. "You're here," she said, smiling. "Come in."

She got up to meet him, the baby still in her arms. She swung the child in front of her; the baby laughed. "He's just being silly," Magdalena said. "He's not hungry any more. He's just playing."

She glanced around, and seeing no one around, gave him a kiss on the cheek. "Sit down," she said. "I'll be done in just a second." She put the bottle on a table and placed the baby on his belly on a mat on the floor. She patted the baby's back to quiet him down. Two other babies were sleeping, one of them snoring softly.

"I'm glad you're here," she said when the baby settled down.

"I have to leave soon."

"Oh," she said, dejected. "Guam?" she continued, in a hopeful tone. He shook his head. "Nam."

"And you can't tell me where in Vietnam you're going," she said in a resigned tone. She sat down beside him and glanced out the window at a bougainvillea vine struggling to survive the city's polluted air.

"Top secret." Nathan could not say he would be part of a forty-plane strike into North Vietnam, to the Haiphong harbor, where Russian and Chinese ships docked and which was therefore a major military supply source. He could not tell her that after a briefing, he and his squadron would leave, and then in Nam they would be joined by a number of fighter planes. Some of the fighter planes would fly ahead to knock out SAM sites that might affect the B-52s. Early in the morning, the forty planes would launch against heavily defended Haiphong to hit truck parts, SAM sites, AAA emplacements, storage areas, and other military targets.

"Do you want something cold to drink?" she offered.

He shook his head and glanced at his watch. "I can't stay long."

"When will you be back?"

"I'll try and get back Thursday for your birthday."

"I hate it when you're gone," she said.

"I'll be back soon."

"I always imagine the worse. All the news about Vietnam, I can't help it. But you will be back Thursday — won't you?"

"I'll try." He had been hiding the small package, but now he handed it to her. "This is for you, in case I don't make it back."

She turned the small package in her hands. It was wrapped in red shiny paper with a large gold bow that had been squashed.

"Open it."

"Now?"

"I want to see if you like it."

She removed the ribbon and peeled off the wrapping and opened a jewelry box. Inside lay a gold bracelet with little animal charms. She smiled and lifted the bracelet so the charms dangled and swayed. She had the sensation of being a child and looking at a new toy for the first time.

"Try it on," he said.

"It's not too young for me?" Her eyes sparkled with delight at the little gold animal charms.

"Absolutely not," he said. "The charms remind me of you. See the goldfish? It's jointed. And there's one of a monkey. Of a turtle too. I thought of you when I saw the bracelet. The children will love it," he said, looking at the sleeping infants on the mats on the floor.

The goldfish wobbled and caught the sun's rays. She sucked in her breath. "It's pretty," she said. "Where did you find it?" She put it on her left wrist; he helped her with the clasp.

"Near the Cholon district."

She lifted her left arm in the air and shook the bracelet so the charms scattered little shards of sunlight all around them.

"The last time I was in Saigon, I saw a woman wearing one just like it."

"Where?" she asked, looking at him from the corner of her eyes.

"At the Cercle de Sportiff Club. We were with some USAID guys, talking shop."

"I see."

"Aren't you going to ask what we talked about?"

"Okay, what did you talk about?"

"We had this heavy discussion about why, except for the Civil War, why the United States fights its wars in other people's backyards. Important stuff like that."

" And the woman, was she part of your group?"

"Oh, no. She was with another woman. They were having lunch. We were all out on the terrace, near the pool."

"So that's what you do when you're away? Having lunch by the pool of a club."

"No, that's not what I always do when I'm away." He laughed, chucking her chin.

She smiled, embarrassed at his gesture of intimacy. "So what happened?"

"To what?"

"The woman . . . the bracelet."

"Nothing. She and her friend were eating and I noticed her bracelet."

"You were looking at her."

"Just her bracelet."

"Was she pretty?"

"One question at a time. You asked what happened. When they were having their coffee, I went to their table and asked her where she got it."

"You did not."

"I introduced myself first."

"She may have thought you were picking her up. Was she pretty?"

"Slender, with hair down to her waist. She was wearing a red *oa dais*."

"A red *oa dais* — how exotic. Was she pretty?"

He paused, puckered his lips as if in deep thought. "If I answer that question, I could get in trouble."

"She was pretty then."

"I was interested only in her bracelet. I went up to her and said, 'I'm sorry to bother you and your friend, but I couldn't help noticing your bracelet. Do you mind if I ask where you got it? I'd like to get one for my fiancee.'"

"Was she . . . beautiful?"

"I'm not going to answer that question."

"Did you really say 'fiancee'?"

"Yes, I did. She spoke French. Her English was not too great, but we managed to communicate. She figured that all I wanted was the name of the store. That same day I went to the Cholon district. Do you like it?"

She lifted her left arm and moved her hands back and forth so the charms clicked together. "It makes me feel sixteen."

"Good."

"I'm not sixteen. Do you know that in the Chinese way of counting, I'll be twenty-seven? How old was the woman in the red *oa dais*?"

"Older than you."

"And pretty, she was pretty, wasn't she? That's why you won't tell me."

"Not pretty at all. She had warts all over her face."

She made a face and laughed. "What's Saigon like? Tell me what it's like."

"Saigon is . . . Saigon. It's a city, and it's crowded. There are motorbikes, jeeps, trucks, taxicabs, and *xich-los*. You have the Cercle Sportif Club where you can have an elegant chateaubriand meal; and then you have the Thanh-Bich Restaurant where you can eat *com be tet*, brown fried rice and a small piece of steak with a large egg over the top, mixed vegetables, a bowl of greens, and *nuoc-mam* fish sauce to pour over everything. It's just Saigon."

"Is it safe there?"

"As safe as Ubec."

"Not that safe then. You have to know where to go and where not to go."

"It's safe enough."

"I'll wait for you Thursday."

"Don't wait for me. I may be late."

"I will wait for you."

"Has anyone ever told you how bullheaded you can be?"

"What time, Thursday?"

"I'm not sure. Late, if we leave that day. But I may have to go to Bien-Hoa, so don't wait for me."

"Thursday, then, on my birthday. I'll see you on my birthday."

"I'll try. I'll see you when I get here. I love you. Do you love me?"

"You know I do. Don't kiss me, someone may see us. But I love you. I'll wait for you."

Nathan left, carrying with him the image of Magdalena seated by the window, holding the baby. It was the last image that stayed with him even as the North Vietnamese fighter planes hit his B-52.

Captive
by Nathan Spencer

crouched in this
four by four box
which my captors
created
i soar
above
the rice paddies
and dense trees
over seas
to memories of
a woman whose
face grows more vivid
as jungle days crawl by
images that feed
a shrunken stomach
that deafen screams   the memory of her
and dull thuds   strand of hair
of rifle butts   curled around
i am not afraid   her neck
                        etched hard
                        the whorls of her fingertips
                        the feel of them
                        against my hungry lips
                        loom above this
                        tight coffin
                        my spine curved
                        for weeks
                        but
                        my spirit
                        remains
                        unfurled

Saturday Down By the Beach

All he had left which they could not imprison was his mind. He would go through the times-table; he would do the alphabet backwards; he would sing and recite poems; and he would remember.

One night when the moon was large, before they became lovers, he caught her flutter past his window. She headed for a huge rock at the edge of the sea where she sat and stared out at the bay. Moonlight shimmered on the water and on her, and for a long while she sat so perfectly still that Nathan felt he was in a dream. She bowed her head, wrapped her arms around herself and rocked herself in a rhythmic way.

He wondered if she might hurt herself and he hurried out the cabaña toward the sea. By the time he made it to the coconut grove, she'd left the rock and was in the water. She was swimming boldly, heading towards the deep. The sea had turned choppy; an undertow or whirlpool could pull her in. He considered calling her, but stopped himself. He must have stayed hidden behind the bushes for a hour, keeping vigil to make sure she was all right.

After that incident, the next time he saw her was at another cove. Saturday morning, the same day he got a copy of *Time* with the cover showing Vietnamese civilians in a burning village. Some were dead, many bleeding. He had seen numerous pictures of Vietnam but this one stayed with him so that even the minutest details were etched in his mind. The village had been bombed, and the people's houses were on fire, all their belongings destroyed no doubt; but worst of all was the look of the people's faces, that look of horror and confusion.

The image would not fade. He decided to go scuba diving. He headed for the cove tucked away on the other side of the island. The trail was rugged and the climb down so steep that he was surprised to find Magdalena at the bottom of the cliff. She was spreading her towel on the sand, her back to him.

She turned when she heard him. "What are you doing here?" she asked, a shadow crossing her face.

"I wanted to ask you the same thing."

"This is my cove. I come here to be alone."

He didn't miss what she said and her petulance annoyed him. "And I'd called this my cove," he said, shifting his gear on his shoulders, ready to leave.

She dug her right foot into the sand. "I was hoping to be alone," she said, her voice softer.

"I can find my way back." He started to walk away.

"I didn't mean it that way. I was just thinking, about things. Stay. I'll show you something," she offered.

He stopped and returned to her.

"Do you know about the cave?" she asked.

He shook his head.

"Very few people do. My father and I used to come here," Magdalena explained. "When I was a child, we found a cave on the other side, high up on the cliff. My father had a story about the cave. He said it was an ancient burial ground. People talk of finding a coffin with a seven-foot skeleton there. Do you want to see it?"

They rented an outrigger from a fisherman and paddled around the cove to the other side where the water was more rough and where sheer cliffs met the sea. The cave was fifteen feet above the cliff. They tied the outrigger to a protruding rock and barefoot, they climbed the rocks to the entrance of the cave. The opening of the cave was narrow and low, and even by the entrance they could feel the moist air from the cave. Without entering, they peered in. The cave was dark but they could make out pottery shards and wood planks scattered about in disarray.

"People have taken away things," she explained. "When I was little, there used to be wooden coffins stacked by the sides of the cave. They were very old. I remembered wanting to bring a piece of it for my science class, but my father said that was bad luck and that I would be desecrating this place. Now they're all gone. This place is like a holy place to me. This was our secret place, my father and I."

"Where you close to him?"

She nodded. "He used to read to me when I was little, children's books, fairy tales, that sort of thing. He helped me with my homework every night. He died a few years ago, but I still miss him. Were you close to your father?"

Nathan paused and looked out at the open sea before answering. "My father was an artist."

"A difficult man, then."

He laughed. "Yes, one could say that about my father."

"My grandfather was a poet. Poets, artists, they're all the same. They have their own world, and they have a difficult time adjusting to the real world."

"You've described my father pretty much."

"I see."

"My sisters and I were close to my mother. She was a quiet, down-to-earth person, very devoted to us."

"You followed me to the sea, the other night. Why did you do that?"

He felt his face flush with embarrassment. "I was worried."

"Of what?" she said.

"That you might hurt yourself."

"I thought of hurting myself, but I saw you and could not do it in front of you."

"I'm glad you changed your mind."

"Do you think you can stop people from hurting?"

He smiled, shrugged his shoulders. "I don't know. I just don't like to see people hurt."

"I see," she said.

They had climbed down and in the outrigger, as they paddled back to the cove, she asked, "Did you like the place?"

"Very much."

"It's a special place, don't you agree? The whole place is like that. They say that at night, enchanted beings swim in the water. Tell me, why did you come here?"

"To think."

"It's a good thinking place. And what did you want to think about?"

"Do you really want to hear about it?"

She nodded.

He took a deep breath, as if to organize his thoughts. "This morning, I saw a picture in a magazine. It was a Vietnamese village."

"Yes, I saw it."

"It bothered me."

"There are many news reports about Vietnam."

"Do you know what I do?" he asked.

"You're a pilot. You work at the base, that is all I know."

"I'm a bomber pilot," he paused. "That is what I do. I was trained to do that, and I'm good at it."

"You're in a war."

"If I had seen that photo last year, I would have echoed my father and said, 'It's a necessary evil.' He was here, in Asia, during World War II. It was a righteous war, his war; the Japanese had been the aggressors. But I've seen Nam and talked to a lot of people, and there's a lot of madness going on. There's some kind of political game going on, and we're counting bodies to prove we're winning so Congress will continue paying for the war. Meanwhile, Vietnamese officers, who are supposed to be our allies, steal supplies and sell these in the blackmarket. It's crazy."

He shook his head and was quiet for a long time. "I can't get over the faces of the people in that picture. We're so far above the ground and what we see is different. The navigator locates the target; the bombardier pushes the button. When we are done, we leave. It's that simple. But it isn't really that simple."

"So you are a man who doesn't want to hurt others. A man who thinks he can stop others from hurting," she said.

"I don't know about that. It's just that the things you see, the things that happen make you think."

By this time, they had reached the cove. After returning the outrigger to the fisherman, Magdalena shook out her towel and settled down to read a book. Nathan did some scuba diving. He found an enormous spiny shell that he brought to shore to show to her.

She ran her finger gently along the brown stripes of the shell. "It's alive, and still young," she said, pointing at the white flesh of the animal. "It's pretty, and if you really want it, I can get Constanzio to bury the shell in sand so ants will eat the flesh of the animal. The ants eat everything." She furrowed her brows slightly. "Constanzio can paint some lacquer on the shell to give it sheen. That way you could keep it as a souvenir, if that is what you really want. "

He turned the shell over in his hand, studied the brown stripes on the white background, felt a yearning to take this back with him to the States. But he weighed what she said, then decided to return the shell where he got it. She seemed pleased at his decision.

Later, they watched the sun descending into the sea. He told her that sometimes just when the sun touched the sea, there's a flash of color. Barely blinking their eyes, barely breathing, all their attention focused in front of them, they watched the huge sun skim the sea then sink into the horizon. There was no flash of color, and they laughed about that a little.

With the darkening sky above them, they walked back home, clambering up the rocks, walking on the narrow rough trail, and feeling perfect happiness.

Remembering Haddam

Sometimes, in his mind, he would write letters:

Dear Mom,

I've been thinking of the big trip East to visit Dad. I never really talked about it, beyond the standard, everything was fine. We didn't talk too much then. I was six but I remember the trip clearly. Aunt Em drove for five days to get us to Connecticut. It was April after Easter, and there was still snow on the ground. Anne and I played with the patches of snow. Ravelle hated it; there it was, spring, but the trees were gray sticks and it was around 35 degrees. For the first few days, she stayed indoors. Grandma Mary jokingly called her a California Girl, like you. Ravelle, four at the time, ran around introducing herself as "a California Girl." Eventually, Ravelle became braver and went outside. The house was terribly drafty anyway. Sometimes it felt warmer outside than in, even though the heater was on and the fire in the fireplace going.

I took it that Grandma was being nice, when she made the "California Girl" reference about you. I was too young to catch nuances of any sort. Grandma seemed to like you; she seemed to blame Dad for your separation. Dad wasn't an easy person, was he? He was the only father I had, so I couldn't compare him with anyone else. There was the constant brooding, and things were never right, not at work, not at home; and he had a way of dominating our lives, so that if he was unhappy we all had to go down with the sinking ship, and more often than not, he was unhappy. When he left us, I wanted him back. I used to pray every night that he'd come home. I got what I wanted. I didn't know then the saying about being careful about what you want because you might get it. I didn't know the price he exacted from those who lived with him.

You have repeatedly told me to forgive and forget; and I admire your ability to have done just that. You managed to make a life with him and to go on with your life after he died. I don't feel I have gaping wounds in me, but I feel — well, a lot of feelings — sadness for one thing, and regret, and pity, and anger. And yes, love. Lots of love for Dad, even though I never told him that. It's easier to forgive and forget a stranger with whom you have no true emotional bonds. But family? It would take a lifetime to sort out the range of emotions one feels for one's family. I have never quite come to terms with my feelings for him, but recently, or at least since his death, I've tried to understand him a little bit better.

That visit made me understand some of Dad's conflicts. Grandma and Grandpa weren't bad people, but they were fixed in their ways. Very precise, and terribly practical. (It's their Yankee way, you used to say.) They had their own ideas about how life ought to be lived; and Dad had other ideas. The irony of it was that he ran away from the kind of life that his parents prescribed, only to end up as a postman, the kind of life Grandpa approved of — "Nice, secure job, why during the depression, mailmen were the envy of everybody."

In Haddam, Grandpa took us around to see places. Once, he brought us to cemeteries to show us the gravestones of his dead relatives. That really made an impression on me, especially his story about the first Spencer in America, Daniel, who came from England as an eight-year-old boy. He had probably been kidnapped in Essex. He worked as an indentured servant in Hartford, and later as a young man, joined others to found Haddam. He had two wives, eight children. One of them was James, who had Oliver, who had Nathan, who had George, and so on til you got to Grandpa, and Dad. Just like the bible. Grandpa knew them all, some seventeen names, from the seventeenth-century all the way to the present.

Ravelle, Anne, and I thought this was wonderful; other grandfathers take their children to Disneyland, not cemeteries. We tried to read the faded gravemarkers. We laughed at some of the names: Aristobulos, Othiel, Mehetable. What kind of name is that? Anne howled, everytime we found another strange name. (Bible names, Grandpa explained.) Ravelle cried over the gravemarkers for the children, smaller stone markers lined up in rows near their parents' gravestones.

Grandpa showed us the tombstones of the Spencers who had been soldiers. They were marked especially, with the American flag and brass inscriptions saying when and where they had fought. He said many Spencers had served their country, and he went on and talked about one's obligation to one's country. I was impressed and I asked Grandpa about the Spencers who had fought during the Civil War, the Spanish American War, and so on. Grandpa was so proud of them that I wanted to be a soldier too, to make people proud of me.

We were all having a good time but when Grandpa started talking about a particular Spencer who had died during World War II, Dad's mood turned. You could see it happening; a scowl crossed his face, his neck and shoulders tensed. Anne and I spotted it right away and we became quiet. Dad snapped at Grandpa saying he'd done his part for his country. Grandpa said, sure he did, in his measured way of talking, and he went on to tell us about other dead relations. Dad didn't leave the matter there. In that garroulous tone of his, he accused Grandpa of never acknowledging his service in the army, that Grandpa never gave him much credit for anything. They had quite a quarrel out in that old cemetery. It was mid-afternoon and the wind was blowing. The coats we had really weren't warm enough for that weather. Anne turned her attention to the melting mounds of snow. Ravelle, who may have forgotten how Dad could get, started to get agitated. I thought she'd cry, but instead she pulled me over to where the crocusses were trying to burst out of the cold soil. She asked me if those were the dead people growing out of the cemetery. I told her no, and I talked to her about the bulbs sleeping during the winter, and that even though they appeared dead, they weren't really dead, and that in the spring, they come out of the soil.

Dad left. In a huff. He was going to walk the three miles home. Grandpa shrugged him off as moody. The three of us children laughed at that word "moody." It was such an understatement. Dad hadn't seen his children in over a year and we were together, having a good time, and he'd gone ahead and ruined everybody's time.

Grandpa must have been used to Dad because he just shined him on. He went on with his tour. He took us to Nathan Hale's red schoolhouse, on the hill overlooking another cemetery. That's when I memorized Nathan Hale's words: "I only regret that I have but one life to give to my country." The words rolled in my tongue. Wonderful words. I thought it was great that after graduating from Yale, he taught at East Haddam schoolhouse. Then he joined the revolutionaries and the British killed him; he was only twenty-one. His name was Nathan, like mine. He was my hero. Between the soldier-Spencers and Nathan Hale, I too wanted to give up my life for my country. I wanted to be like Nathan Hale and I wanted to be remembered like the Spencers with the special gravemarkers. I'm ashamed to admit that I did not want to be like Dad, constantly mulling over something, constantly regretting not doing this or that, constantly second-guessing himself. I was thinking more of Superman. Kid stuff. The path to greatness, to nobility was so simple, so easy.

I was six then. I'm no longer six, and things are no longer so simple. It's a cliche but war is not as glorious as it's made out to be. Despite what the movies, books and songs say, war is about pain, death, destruction. I think

Dad knew this. I suspect that Dad knew a lot more than I gave him credit. I never gave him much of a chance, and now he's no longer around to talk to, to ask how things were for him. That's one of my regrets. I only have bits and pieces to go by.

Your Son,
Nathan

Family Cemetery

Several typhoons hit the island of Ubec, one after the other, and Typhoon Mercedes in particular shook the island terribly. The winds uprooted power lines and the city and towns had no electricity for weeks. Sheets of galvanized iron roofing were ripped off houses. Matters were particularly bad in Mantalongon. The farmers' crops were destroyed; the workers at the mines could not work.

Ever since he was a child, Nestor had hated the typhoon season. From July to November, he lived in constant dread, as if something catastrophic would happen. Even before the rains came, he would secure the house — close all windows and doors, do everything he could to keep the rain from getting into the house, which it did anyway, seeping in under crevices and between the roof tiles. To drown the lashing rain and whipping wind, he would turn up the radio; and at night, he would pull the blanket over his head. In Manila, when the winds blew over 100 kilometers per hour and schools and offices shut down, he would stay in his house, cooped up with Cora and the servants. He felt as if he were in a tomb and he would drink to try and rid himself of his sadness. He hated the monsoon season, hated it from the time he was two.

When the rains began he sealed his house as he always did, but he refused to be imprisoned indoors with Cora and April. Even while a typhoon raged, he would slip on his knee-high black rubber boots and black raincoat and leave the house. It was impossible to drive in the muddy, flooded dirt roads of Mantalongon and so he would walk, to the mine sites to check on the men and the progress of their work. Operations were extremely slow because of the water and mud that had to be pumped out of shafts. He would go to the town's open market, hoping to find the vendors with their colorful wares, only to find the stalls deserted. On several occasions he walked to Pagsama Falls, braving the slippery rocks. In the cold, slanting rain with the wind whipping his overcoat, he paused where he and Luisa had been decades ago, and always he felt loss.

Once, he walked up the mountain, past the source of the spring that nourished Pagsama and saw that the trees there had been cut down. When he asked Carding who had logged the area, Carding said Nestor's brother Junior had done it, and that they had meant to replant but never got around to doing it. Nestor studied the barren land; he poked at the loose soil and looked at the rainwater that moved the soil downward. Something inside him clicked, and he recalled the Great Flood of Ormoc.

When he had been Minister of Health, he had to fly to the City of Ormoc that had been the site of major flooding. The mountains above Ormoc had been denuded, from logging as well, and one night during the typhoon season, the river had swollen and rushed down to the city, flooding the city, drowning people, destroying homes. Thousands had died. There were so many corpses that the best they could do was dig out deep pits and have mass burials, which went against the grain of Filipinos who were fond of elaborate funeral rituals. There were many more bodies that could not be recovered, that had washed to the sea. For weeks, people refused to eat the fish, squid, and crabs from the area because they had eaten human flesh.

And now, Nestor could see the same possibility and he told Carding to tell his workers to stay away from the river and its banks, and to warn the people. True enough, one night when the winds and rains lashed at 117 kilometers per hour, the river rose suddenly and water came crashing down, sweeping away houses, vegetation, people, animals, anything along its way. Witnesses reported a loud roaring sound, then muddy water entered homes, shook houses from their foundations, and houses tumbled and disintegrated in the swollen river. Fortunately, because people had been forewarned, no one died.

Still another casualty of the flood was the cemetery located farther down the mountain, in a valley that filled up with riverwater and looked like a lake for a week. When the water subsided, graves were exposed, skeletons and coffins strewn all over the place.

Even before the water at the cemetery dried up, and even before the rains stopped, people were already there. Nestor met Magdalena at the cemetery during this time.

Nestor's mother had been distraught since the flood happened. One of her concerns was that something had happened to Junior's grave. As soon as she could, she had sent some of their men to check on their family mausoleum. The men reported that they were very lucky because their mausoleum was standing and that Jose's and Junior's graves were not damaged. April continued to nag nonetheless until finally Nestor went to the cemetery. Wearing a heavy raincoat and hat, he left his house and slowly made his way through the slippery mountain roads until he reached the cemetery. April had thrust flowers in his hands — roses, dahlias, and babysbreath — and he shook off drops of rain from the flowers when he reached his family's mausoleum. He lay the flowers in front of his father and brother's markers and assessed the situation. He could see that the mausoleum was covered with mud and needed thorough cleaning, that the concrete of one part had chipped off and would have to be fixed, and the whole thing had to be whitewashed. Aside from that, the mausoleum was in relatively good shape. The others were less fortunate; many would not even recover the bones of their ancestors.

He brushed off the dirt in front of the markers and thought he should pray. He paused, trying to bring to mind the memorized prayers of his youth. All he could recall was the Our Father, so he said that three times under this breath — "Our Father, who art in heaven . . ." While praying, he thought of Junior's dream about running down a road to escape something. "Why couldn't you just get off the road?" he muttered, but even as he said that, he knew it wasn't quite so simply. He himself had a recurring dream of running around a racetrack, not running away from something like Junior's dream, but simply running around the same track, over and over again; the metaphor in his own life had not escaped him, he knew what the dream meant.

An image came to him: he and his brother racing through the fields of corn one sweltering summer day, and the long green corn leaves whizzed past them as they ran, breathless, along the narrow trails cutting the fields. He liked that memory and he strained hard to have a pleasant thought of his father. The only image that came to him was that of his father as a young man standing with Juana on the deck of the boat that brought them to Northern Luzon many years ago.

This surprised him and he held it in his mind. He was still deep in this reverie when a woman's voice startled him: "Doctor Hernandez, excuse me."

He opened his eyes and turned to find a woman standing under the rain, umbrella over her head. He had only seen her from the distance, but he knew it was Luisa's daughter, Magdalena.

"Is your aunt here, Sofia?" he asked, looking around.

"No, she left a while ago. I didn't mean to interrupt you. I was visiting my family —" she pointed to a mausoleum in another part of the cemetery. He could see that the Delgado mausolem had been badly damaged by the flood. A huge portion of the mausoleum had crumbled off, and two crypts were gaping empty.

"The Delgados," he said.

She nodded. "We have much to do. We have lost some of our dead. I have been meaning to talk to you. You are a doctor, I understand. My aunt told me about you. And she told me to see you, my condition you understand, and the city is very far away." She rested her left hand on her swollen stomach.

He pointed to the dark clouds overhead. "It will rain harder. We better go."

"The birds were noisy this morning," she said, as they started walking, he leading the way, past skulls and bones that gleamed a strange steel-gray under the rain. Once she almost tripped over a coffin and he extended his right arm to her, and she held it.

"It is terrible, all this. So much suffering. We came to visit our dead. We have lost the bodies of my grandparents. *Tiya* Sofia is inconsolable." She pointed once again at the Delgado mausoleum that was now close by.

They walked to it and paused. Nestor studied the empty crypts. "Roberto and Juana were your grandparents," he said.

"They are the two missing. I have told my aunt it is not so important to actually have their bones here. Other people have lost more. They are dead after all. Besides there is simply nothing we can do. Their remains are gone, the flood took them away."

"He was a poet," Nestor said.

She was surprised. "How did you know that?"

"It's a small town."

She laughed. "They say around here you can't sneeze without people knowing about it."

"I've heard other versions of that saying."

"It's true, isn't it? Mantalongon is a small place. There's something about a small place that can be comforting, but at the same time threatening. I suppose it's because you can't simply disappear. You are always scrutinized, accounted for. It can be a pain sometimes. *Tiya* Sofia mentioned your father's death. I'm sorry. You are old friends of the family, then?"

"My father knew your grandmother."

"Juana. She used to be there." She pointed out Juana's empty crypt, then she pointed to the ground at a grave-marker, which had the carving of a long-haired woman bent over in sorrow. "That was hers. I hardly knew her. She and *Lolo* died when I was little."

"Juana La Guapa because she was beautiful."

"All I've heard is that she was very hard-working and devoted to her family. If I have a daughter I want to name her after her."

"And you haven't heard that your grandfather was a poet?"

"I've heard he was eccentric . . . yes, he was a writer, I believe. I don't know much about them. I have one memory of my grandparents. I must have been only three or four, so I am not sure if it's a real memory. *Lolo* was sitting at his desk, doing something, and *Lola* Juana was bent over, helping him with what he was doing. Mama did not like to come here, and so we did not visit often. I only started to come here several years ago when I ran the monkey business."

They returned to the trail and headed for the main road. The drops of rain grew larger.

"The baby . . ." he started.

"Late September." She paused then continued. "I should tell you Dr. Hernandez, that my relatives are not happy about this child. That is why I am here, not in the city. I don't know if you have heard, but the father of my child may be dead. We are still waiting to know what happened to him exactly."

"I have heard," he said.

"It has been one thing after another. He was a pilot, and his plane had been shot down over North Vietnam. There is nothing definite about what happened to him, if he is dead, or alive. It is difficult not to know. Sometimes, it's almost impossible, but I think of the child, and I know I have to keep on, for the child's sake."

"If the baby's due so soon, wouldn't it have been better . . . what I mean is, there are no facilities here."

"Yes, the city would be better. The city has its plusses, and the city has its minuses. You know how the city is, Doctor, and how people there love to talk." She laughed.

"You mustn't concern yourself with that."

"I don't, but my mother is there and the gossip hurts her. I don't want to embarrass her any more than she already is. I'll stay with my aunt until the baby's due. She needs my help to deal with these matters; we've had some water-damage at home as well. Perhaps by the time the baby's born, we'll already know what happened to him . . . the baby's father, that is. It is difficult to constantly think of him; it is a relief to think of other things, even matters such as this." She gestured at the cemetery, then sighed.

Not knowing what to say, he kept quiet.

"We were talking of getting married, of living in Colorado, but now . . . I don't know. I only wish he were alive. He's listed as M.I.A. but sometimes, they're not really missing. He had told me that sometimes, commanding officers list them that way even though they're dead to give surviving relatives additional benefits. I don't know if this is true. I don't know what to believe. It is difficult not to know. If he had just left me, for whatever reason, that would be easier than this. Even knowing he is dead would be some kind of relief. This uncertainty is difficult."

By this time, they had reached the part of the road where he had to turn left and she right. They stopped.

"Tell your *Tiya* Sofia hello for me. Your mother as well."

She looked surprised. "You know her too? I'll tell them both I saw you. Good-bye for now."

Nestor stood and watched her walk away, her figure turning gray with the rain as the distance between them grew. And inside he felt another tug at his heart, a regret that this handsome and graceful woman could have been his own.

Luisa's Dream
(1968)

Luisa dreamt of a little man carrying a wooden club, and this little man started hitting her with the club. His face was pale, bloodless really, and his veins stuck out like wiggling worms on his forehead and throat. He was ugly, this little man who gritted his teeth as he swung his club. Luisa dodged here and there; she was frantic, trying to protect herself, but his club hit her right cheek, and when she reached up to soothe her face, she discovered that part of her face was missing. She stood on an isolated dirt road, the kind that snaked its way in and out of little barrios, narrow, with potholes and boulders haphazardly sticking up here and there; and along the roadside grew wild bushes bearing fetid-smelling flowers called "goat flowers." With her right hand cradling her face, she wondered what she ought to do, when suddenly little people darted out from behind the bushes. About a dozen of them ran around her, as if they were in great confusion. They were small, like children, but their faces appeared old and contorted, with pits on their skins, and they were wailing high-pitched cries that made the hair on her arms prickle. Luisa looked around, searching for the man with the club, but he had disappeared.

She awoke and her throat was dry. She felt a foreboding, the same feeling she had the day Fermin had died. It was a tension, a darkness, and it sapped her energy. She said her prayers to shake off the feeling, but it persisted.

Later, she dressed in a bright floral dress, which was too frilly for a woman her age, but she slipped it on anyway; and she applied make-up to hide the rings under her eyes. During breakfast, while Rosa whipped up her chocolate drink, Luisa talked about her dream to Rosa, hoping to purge it out of her system, hoping to negate its power. But the more she prattled, the more frightened she became, as if she were a drowning woman thrashing about wildly in the sea, clutching at the air — hopeless.

Luisa's Monologue

Estrella called to say that Magdalena was at the hospital, complications, she said. My thoughts were still on that awful dream about the ugly little man. I didn't think the worst; the baby was born early — that was the problem. After all, there were no medical facilities in Mantalongon. I'll admit that I had been relieved when Magdalena had decided to move there. She was starting to show and it's difficult in Ubec, with those biddies watching, their tongues wagging constantly. It's their fulltime preoccupation, and certainly they watched Magdalena's waist thicken. It was painful for me to know people were talking about us, ridiculing our family. I'd worked hard to protect our family name — Fermin would have been proud of me.

At the hospital, I was totally unprepared to find Magdalena on the emergency bed with tubes running in and out of her face. Her gown was open, exposing her breasts and stomach, still big from carrying the baby.

Doctor Veloso, chief of staff, the best Ubec had to offer, was working on her. With his hands resting at the base of her sternum, he gave a quick push so her body jolted. It took my breath away each time he did that. Another doctor and five medical students hovered around the periphery of the room. There was blood on the sheets, on the bed, on the doctors' hands; and bloody rags lay on the floor as if they had been quickly thrown there to sop up the blood.

Before Doctor Veloso declared her dead, I knew because the little man had already taken away flesh from my flesh. Many, many years ago, during wartime, I had held Magdalena in my arms and I checked her eyes and fingers and toes to see if she was a normal baby — flesh from her flesh — and even while I had been afraid, I gloried in this miracle of life. Magdalena had grown inside my belly, lived off my blood and muscle, thrived on what I had eaten. For nine months the two of us had been one. And now I was staring at my daughter on the hospital bed, a woman I hardly recognized because of the blood and bruises and tubes. The last time I had seen her, she was dressed in a flowing turquoise maternity dress; her belly rounded, and she had pressed my hand against her stomach so I could feel my grandchild kicking. "I'm naming her Juana, after your mother," she said, and the way she had said it made me realize that all along I'd given my mother little credit, that I'd never as much as honored her by naming my child after her.

The doctors took turns pumping her chest. Everytime they pushed, I felt it, felt my heart leap and I prayed that Magdalena's would do the same. An enormous round clock hung on the wall and now and then I would glance at it and suffer the eternity it took for the minute hand to move. I egged them on. She was only twenty-six; she just had a baby; she couldn't die. Not now. Later, when she was old or maybe even when the child was just a bit older, but not now. Surely, they could do something for her? They worked, and continued working, and with every push on Magdalena's chest, I felt my own heart leap. Finally it was the sight of the blue-black marks that made me shake my head and tell them to stop.

There was silence; time was suspended; and for a brief moment, I felt some relief. I pulled her gown up to cover her body and I stroked her hair. And then I noticed that Nestor was there after all, and I wondered what he was doing there, beside Magdalena, my child, his child. He unhooked the tubes and removed her gold bracelet and ring and handed them to me. He had a sad, dark look and I asked, "What are you doing here, Nestor?"

"I delivered the baby, then she started bleeding, and Sofia and I brought her here. Even if she had recovered, her brain would not be right. She had stopped breathing for a long time."

I stared, not comprehending.

"It takes only a few minutes and then it's too late. The mortician will want to know how many days of viewing she'll have."

"The mortician?"

"The embalming, you see."

His words were crude and I stepped away from the bed. What was he doing here anyway? He didn't belong here with us; he could have, once upon a time, if Fate had willed it, he could have been part of us. I wanted to tell him to go away, to go home to his wife. I had managed all this time without him, so who was he to talk about Magdalena's brain and morticians and embalming. He had no idea of what I was going through, of what it felt like to be a parent seeing your daughter dead when the order of things is for the parent to die first. I wanted to tell him I hated him for those words, that I hated him for abandoning me not once but twice, that most of all I hated him for not keeping

Magdalena alive. What kind of doctor was he? Minister of Health, wasn't he? He should have destroyed the little man with the club. He should have saved her; if he could not — did not save me, discarded me in fact — the very least he could have done was save my Magdalena. He owed us that much. But the words were too plentiful and painful and they jammed in my throat.

Estrella held my arm. "It's all right, *Tiya*," she said, "I'll take care of the arrangements. Don't worry too much. There's nothing you can do about it. But the baby's all right, though, healthy as can be. *Tiya* Sofia's with her at the nursery."

"Juana," I said.

Estrella looked at me questioningly.

"That's the name Magdalena chose. We'll name her Juana."

"Of course, *Tiya*. That's a pretty name. It's a good thing Dr. Hernandez was there to deliver the baby. There was no one else who could help in Mantalongon."

"He didn't save her."

"He did all he could, *Tiya*"

"He should have given her his blood, his heart, anything to keep her alive."

"It happened during the night, *Tiya* and the storm was very bad. It was too dangerous to travel in the dark. They had to wait for dawn, when there was enough light."

"He is always too late," I said brusquely.

Time took on a strange quality. We had been in the emergency room, then we were downstairs near a driveway. Nestor and two medical students appeared, pushing a gurney with a figure covered with a white sheet. A piece of white paper was pinned to the sheet, and on the paper was scrawled: Magdalena Sotelo.

Strange what you remember under stress — I recall that half-a-sheet of paper fluttering while the men struggled to transfer her body to the funeral car. They pushed and lifted and rolled her body, and once the sheet slipped off her foot and I saw that her toes had turned dark purple.

All the way to Cosmopolitan Funeral Parlor, I worried that she was cold. It was a thought I could not shake off even when the funeral home's director greeted us. He was a big man with beads of perspiration on his forehead. "How many days, Mrs. Sanchez?" he asked, with a tone of impatience.

"It just happened today. She died this morning."

"I mean, how many days of viewing do you want?" He mopped his face with his handkerchief.

Estrella stepped forward. "Just a few days, don't you agree Dr. Hernandez?" Estrella said.

"Ah, a doctor," the director said, turning to Nestor, waiting for him to cut the matter short.

"Are there relatives far away who need to travel? We can make it a week in that case," Nestor said.

Estrella answered. "Some aunts in Manila and Baguio. There is no need to prolong it. It's more difficult if it drags on. In my case with Mariquita, I wanted it finished as soon as possible."

The funeral director twirled his thumbs impatiently. "There are others waiting, Doctor."

Nestor turned to me. "Is that what you want? Three or four days? It is the last time, after that, it is over."

"I don't know. I cannot think. Whatever Estrella decides is fine. It doesn't matter. Enough time for her family and friends to see her and say goodbye. That is all." How weightless I felt. I took several deep breaths and stared out the window at the busy street. It was now drizzling. Nestor and Estrella conferred with the director, then Estrella returned to ask about insurance.

"Doesn't she have insurance, *Tiya*? Do you remember after *Tiyo* died, she decided to get insurance? I'm sure she did. Was that Prudential? I think it was Prudential. She mentioned it to me in passing. Do you know where her papers are?"

I pulled myself away from the soft raindrops outside. I had to stop and think, and unable to come up with an answer, realized how little I knew about my daughter's affairs—how little I knew about my daughter after all. I shook my head.

"Never mind, *Tiya*, I'll call Prudential."

The secretary handed me a piece of paper. "Mrs. Sanchez, could your write down information about your daughter. For the obituary."

Pen in hand, I started: Magdalena Sanchez Sotelo, born December 30, 1942 in Maibog, Leyte, died September 28, 1968 in Ubec City, Beloved Daughter, Wife, Mother, Lover, Known by all as Magdalena.

What else could I say about my daughter? How could I sum her up in a few lines? What could I write down? Could I mention that she had been a quiet, charming child but terribly spoiled by Fermin? Could I say that Magdalena broke my heart and Fermin's several times by her willfulness? Could I say that I, Luisa, loved my flesh-of-my-flesh and how sorry I was that I never showed this love enough, that I never told her about this love at all? Could I confess that I Luisa was angry that I had this inability to forgive, to forget, to truly love?

I was still staring at the paper when Nestor returned. "Luisa," he said, "there is the business of . . . it's a terrible matter . . . but you need to choose a coffin."

I had gone through this with Fermin, only, in Fermin's case it had been Magdalena who had accompanied me upstairs, past the altars with coffins and mourners sitting in benches, eating, gambling, praying. It had been Magdalena who had selected the steel-gray coffin, "simple but elegant" for Fermin. Now, Nestor and I walked past rows of brand-new coffins.

"Look at this," I said, making a face at a fushcia-colored coffin. "What a terrible color really. I wouldn't be caught dead — well, that's not the right thing to say, is it?" I said and a quick laugh passed between my lips.

The director rattled off prices as he pointed out coffins.

"It does not matter. Anything, anything at all. Whatever it costs is fine."

"Insurance will pick up some of the expenses. It's not necessary to be extravagant Luisa," Nestor said.

"Something elegant and simple," I replied.

"This gray one, with a bit of silver. What do you think?"

"That's fine. Fermin was buried in a gray coffin as well."

"I'm sorry, I didn't mean to bring that up —"

"The gray with silver will do," I told the director. "Just add it all up."

"Yes, of course. With the flowers and services, and we'll send the bill to the insurance agent and the balance to Madam. After the funeral, of course."

Downstairs, the secretary informed us that Estrella was in the embalming room. "Do you want to see her? The embalming room is in the back of the building," the secretary said.

I scanned Nestor's face for an answer.

"Let's see what they need. They might need her clothes."

We took a side passageway to the back wing of the building. Near the entrance Nestor told me to wait. He entered and as the door swung open, I caught a glimpse of rows of marble slabs.

"Beth is bringing over Magdalena's dress. Peach-colored, I believe. Silk. Is that all right with you?" he said, when he returned.

I nodded. It was a dress made by Pitoy, very expensive, and it looked it, in its elegant simplicity.

"Your niece wants to put pearls on her, but I warned her to be sure and remove it before the burial. There are grave robbers."

"Yes. Can I see her now?"

He shook his head. "Not yet. Wait until she's ready."

Later I saw her lying on the marble slab, clothed in the peach silk dress, her face was made-up. Only her hair, which had not been combed, showed signs of distress. Strands of matted black hair against shiny stone. The contrast of the black against the white marble fascinated me. It was easier to look at her hair rather than her face that was so strangely still. I could not help herself, I reached out and stroked her cheek but quickly drew back because she was so cold, as cold I imagined as the marble underneath her. There was no blood this time, unlike the emergency room that had been drenched in blood. Things had been cleaned up: no blood on her face, none on her body, and the terrible bruises on her chest were covered by the designer silk dress, hidden forever so she almost looked like she was asleep.

"Don't worry about her hair, *Tiya*. She has to be transferred, so they'll wait until she's in . . . you know . . . the coffin. We have her shoes, but we didn't put them on. It's not good to put shoes on the dead, otherwise they'll walk the earth forever. We'll put them beside her feet. No one can see them. There are so many things to remember. Her rosary has to be cut." Estrella's voice echoed in the mortuary.

"What rosary, Estie?" I asked.

"The rosary she'll be holding. It needs to be cut, otherwise bad luck will go around in the family. God knows we've had our share."

"They're just superstitions, Luisa. If you don't believe in them, just say so, and they'll do what you want," Nestor said.

"It won't hurt her if we do all that," I said.

"Me, my attitiude is: why not? Even though I believe in the Lord, I follow these beliefs. I did them with Mariquita. She didn't wear her shoes; and her rosary was also cut."

"Then fine, don't put her shoes on and cut the rosary."

The funeral director who had left the embalming room returned with a companion. They were wheeling a steel-gray coffin into the room. The director's eyes rested on me. Nestor, catching his glance, quickly asked me to leave. "They have to move her body."

He led me outside, under an overhang to protect me from the rain. When the mortuary doors closed, the sounds from the embalming room became muffled and the noise of the rain and traffic rose around us. The plaintive cry of a *balut* vendor echoed above all other sounds.

"Do you hear him? He's still working even with this rain," I said. "Magdalena hated *balut*; she could not stand to look at the duck's embryo. It's such an ugly-looking thing after all, with big eyes and feathers. Tell me, Nestor, did she suffer?"

"No more than usual."

"Did she have a hard time?"

"No, the baby came normally. It was the bleeding that was problem. I couldn't stop it. I'm sorry, Luisa."

"I can't imagine that there was nothing you could do to help her. Was there no medicine to stop bleeding? A shot. Pills. Something."

"I didn't even have ice, Luisa. Sofia was with me, she can vouch that I did everything I could."

"I shouldn't blame you, Nestor, but I can't even imagine she's gone. Yesterday, she was alive; now everything is changed. She is all I have."

"The baby is there."

"Yes, the baby. If she had stayed in the city, Nestor, would she have lived?"

"That's a difficult question, Luisa. No one has the answer."

"I don't know what to do, Nestor. I feel crazy. What did you do after your father died?"

"There were many things to do. There were a lot of adjustments."

"But inside, what did you do inside?"

"It's not easy and you try to deal with it. One day you'll surprise yourself and find you can laugh again."

"That sounds like such a cliche, Nestor, like one of your old lines. I don't think this pain will ever go away. Or perhaps you're stronger than me. Maybe you have the ability to lose people you love and simply forget them. You have certainly proven that."

"No, I don't have that ability, Luisa."

"You don't forget then. You have not forgotten."

"I have not forgotten."

"Not even Maibog, Nestor?"

"Especially Maibog."

"There was a time I thought you had forgotten and I hated you then, Nestor."

"I'm sorry to hear that."

"You promised, you see, you said you'd come back."

"It was wartime, Luisa."

"I waited for you. It was difficult for me, Nestor. I waited."

"It was impossible to see you. I was in Mindanao until the end of the war."

There was silence during which our minds must have locked on fragments of past longings, yearnings that had become diffused and vague with time.

"Did your wound heal properly?" I finally said.

"Sometimes when it rains, it hurts, but it's not hurting now."

"They say that happens, some kind of arthritis."

"After the war I wanted to see you, but you had a child, and I decided to leave you alone. We've certainly messed up our lives, haven't we?"

"You have messed up your life, Nestor. Not me."

"That is true."

"I don't know what to do, Nestor. I keep thinking: if only she had stayed here in the city, she'd be fine; if only the weather had not been so bad and she could have returned here on time, she'd be fine; if only you had done everything you could, she'd be fine. She was such a pretty baby, Nestor. You should have seen her. She wasn't bald like some babies; she had hair and a pretty little face. She looked perfect, like a doll, and she had such a nice disposition. Fermin was so enchanted with her. They were close, those two. And they're both gone. I'm alone. It hurts, Nestor, inside. It's a pain I never knew existed."

"You're not alone. Many people love you. I love you."

For a moment I was tempted to confess to him that Magdalena was his daughter, but there was too much ground to cover, too many lives that would be upturned; and so I remained quiet, as I had these past twenty-seven years.

Sometime later, at the nursery, Sofia hugged me, and showed me Magdalena's baby, my granddaughter. Juana was swaddled in a light cotton blanket so only her little round face showed. Although asleep, her mouth made sucking motions. Her eyelashes were dark and long and formed little crescents against her cheeks.

I picked her up and felt her weight, smelled the scent of talcum powder and of something sweet that I could not identify. She gave a deep sigh; I stroked her face.

"She's a beautiful baby, Luisa. Strong. She'll make it," Sofia said.

"Will I forget, Sofia? Will I forget his pain?"

Sofia, still wearing black for the boy she loved half-a-century ago gave a wan smile. "No, but you cannot not dwell on it; you have your grandchild to think about."

"Yes," I said, and I looked at the child and saw in her face traces of my Magdalena. And I knew I had to be brave and survive her funeral and the long days ahead because Magdalena's child was now in my hands.

Epilogue

With the help of my aunt, my grandmother raised me. After my mother's death, she moved out of her house and we lived in my mother's house by the sea, the house with the beautiful cabaña that had been home to my father for a little while. In the backyard the pond with koi remained, and my grandmother said that my mother's beloved monkey on the verandah survived until I was three.

My grandmother lived to see me married — happily, I might add; and shortly before she had her heart attack, I had told her that if I have a daughter, I would name her Magdalena. She smiled when I said that, even as tears filled her eyes.

My father remains a P.O.W. There are many times when I dream of him striding down the walkway to find me, his daughter. The other image I have of him is this: when he died, the second his soul left his body, my mother was there to welcome him with outstretched arms.

Love like that is eternal.

Juana

About the Writer

Cecilia Manguerra Brainard is the author and editor of ten books, including the internationally-acclaimed novel, *When the Rainbow Goddess Wept, Acapulco at Sunset and Other Stories, Philippine Woman in America,* and *Woman with Horns and Other Stories.* **Magdalena** is her second novel. She edited *Fiction by Filipinos in America and Contemporary Fiction by Filipinos in America.* She co-edited two children's books and *Journey of 100 Years: Reflections on the Centennial of Philippine Independence.*

Cecilia has received numerous awards for her literary achievements and for the service she has given her Filipino and Filipino American communities. In 1998, she received the Outstanding Individual Award from her birth city, Cebu, Philippines. She has also received a California Arts Council Fellowship in Fiction, a Brody Arts Fund Award, a Special Recognition Award from the Los Angeles City Board of Education for her work dealing with Asian American youths. In 2001, she received a Filipinas Magazine Award for Arts, and a Certificate of Recognition from the California State Senate, 21st District.

She teaches writing at UCLA-Extension and University of Southern California.

She has a website at http://www.ceciliabrainard.com. She is married to Lauren R. Brainard, a former Peace Corp Volunteer to the Philippines; they have three sons.